# THE SITTING DUCK

## By George Bagby

# THE SITTING DUCK

GEORGE BAGBY

PUBLISHED FOR THE CRIME CLUB BY
DOUBLEDAY & COMPANY, INC.
GARDEN CITY, NEW YORK
1981

All of the characters in this book
are fictitious, and any resemblance
to actual persons, living or dead,
is purely coincidental.

Library of Congress Cataloging in Publication Data

Bagby, George, 1906–
The sitting duck.

I. Title.
PS3537.T3184S55     813'.52
ISBN 0-385-17802-6     AACR2
Library of Congress Catalog Card Number 81–43251

*First Edition*

*For*
*Michele Tempesta*
*great editor and good friend*
*with*
*the author's*
*esteem and affection.*

# THE SITTING DUCK

# CHAPTER 1

Jack Sterling was the impossible bird. No ornithologist could ever believe him. Sterling was a canary, but he was also a sitting duck. In the world of ornithological classification it is obvious that no canary could ever be a duck; but in the world of metaphor—underworld metaphor and police metaphor—canaries are all too likely to be sitting ducks. Every effort had been made to save Jack Sterling from any such ornithological doubling, but when a bird won't cooperate, there isn't much that can be done for him.

It began five years back, or at least that was when I first had any knowledge of Jack Sterling. I came to know of him through my old friend, Inspector Schmidt. The inspector is the NYPD's chief of Homicide, and as you probably know, this won't be the first time I will have written an account of one of Schmitty's murder investigations.

It had been then, five years before, that Sterling had done his singing. The burden of his song touched only tangentially on murder. It might be said, therefore, that with the canary the inspector was only tangentially involved, but Schmitty's involvement with murder is never tangential. It had been a big story in its time, but you know how it is with big stories: Last year's big story becomes this year's dim memory. After five years who will remember?

Not the people who heard about it on the TV evening news or who read about it in their morning papers, but there will be a few who do remember. So there were those few who even after five years remembered Jack Sterling and the songs he sang. There were those who had suffered as a result of his singing, and there was Inspector Schmidt. There has never been anyone or anything having to do with murder that the inspector has forgotten. There was also me, George Bagby, but I only happened to remember.

So far as the murder part of the affair had gone, for the inspector it had been nothing more than a bit of dull routine. There had never been any question of finding the killer or of proving the killing on him. That much of it had been open and shut, but that doesn't say it hadn't been peculiar. The victim was a police officer. The killer was a laundryman.

It began as a turning-worm story. Small businessman, held up at gun point once too often, takes to keeping a loaded revolver under the counter. The next stick-up man who walks into his laundry and pulls a gun on him gets it between the eyes.

How could the small businessman have known that the gun pulled on him was a police .38? Would you believe that a moonlighting cop could be running a side line of knocking off laundries? You wouldn't. No more would our small businessman.

No more would Inspector Schmidt. There's nothing he would like better than to believe that every cop is a good cop, but he knows better and he is resigned to the knowledge. A rogue cop was never an impossibility. The inspector, nevertheless, didn't believe that small businessman. It wasn't his loyalty to the men on the force—although it has always been great—that swayed his thinking. It was that he knew too much about rogue cops, and he was unable to fit the laundryman's story to anything he knew.

When a police officer goes wrong, he is most likely to take the shakedown route. Robbery at the point of a service revolver has never been rogue-cop style. So Inspector Schmidt had his doubts, but there was every reason to have expected that he would remain with them. At that stage the whole matter had been handled in precinct. Chief of Homicide Schmidt had as routine seen the precinct reports, and he hadn't liked them. The thing, however, hadn't been in his lap. It had been in the hands of the DA's office.

Bringing the man to trial, they would have been up against a plea of self-defense. As things turned out, it didn't happen that way. Jack Sterling came into the picture. He was arrested on an assault charge, and his victim was another small businessman. Sterling was an enforcer for a shake-down gang, and when the DA's men got on him, he sang. Never has there been the canary that sang louder or longer, and few have sung as effectively.

He brought down the whole operation. He blew the whistle on a few heavyweight gangland characters, but it didn't stop there. Sterling read out chapter and verse on a covey of FBI agents and on some half a dozen NYPD cops. Among the latter was that officer the little laundryman had knocked off.

The little man went to trial with his self-defense story wrecked, but it made little difference. The prosecuting attorney could tell the jury that when someone tries to shake a good citizen down, the good citizen doesn't go to a gun. He goes to the law. The jury inevitably asked itself what law—It was a representative of the law who had been shaking him down. The laundryman got off. Cops went to jail, FBI agents went to jail, the careers of both were down the drain. The gangland lugs, even the heavyweights, also went to jail, but for them, of course, that meant only an intermission in their careers, if even that. The executive types all too often just go on running things from the pokey.

Jack Sterling, however, had made a deal. The Feds took on the job of protecting him. When he had finished his song and he had done all the necessary testifying, he had been whisked secretly out of New York, transported elsewhere, and given a brand new identity. Jack Sterling, as Jack Sterling, had ceased to exist. It was to have been expected that he would never be seen in New York again.

When I did see him, therefore, recognition was something less than immediate. It had been five years, and even then he had, as I said, impinged on Inspector Schmidt only tangentially, and then in a case that didn't have enough in it to make it worth writing about. The only reason why I had any memory of the man was that back then, five years before, his incongruity had haunted me.

It had been his looks. I don't know that I have ever seen a face that could have stood more tellingly as a representation of gentleness and purity. The guy was an enforcer. He earned his cakes and ale by slapping people around and that only as a preface to breaking arms or smashing knee caps, and he walked around behind the cloyingly sweet face of one of the gentler saints in a Mannerist painting.

It was a memorable face. You don't see many men with faces that strongly suggestive of an overripe peach. That it should have been Jack Sterling's face, I had found staggering. So I happened to remember.

The place where I saw him was also an impediment to recognition. That I'd had no possible expectation of ever again seeing the man in New York was only part of it. I saw him in a New York watering spot that I would have sworn had never been frequented by the likes of Jack Sterling. It was one of the P.J. places. The area known as the fashionable East Side is peppered with them. They call themselves by one Irish surname or another prefaced by the P.J. initials. They are cocktail-lounge emasculations of Irish saloons. The P.J. may stand for pajamas since the distaff segment of their clientele tends toward frequenting the joints in the lounging variety.

The one where I saw Jack Sterling is on the avenue just around the corner from my apartment. Proximity is the only thing that ever brings me there. I have never felt that it has anything going for it but that it is the nearest oasis. Young Wall Streeters and young advertising executives plus some of the same ilk who refuse to recognize aging come home from the office to do a quick switch into the brand-name jeans and the gold chains and then nip around to this local P.J. The bar does a big business in white wine by the glass and Perrier with a twist.

You can pop in there for a serious drink, and I occasionally do, but it's no place where I ever settle in for an evening of serious drinking, and I'm not even an enforcer with that face of a Mannerist saint. When I first saw him, therefore, although I registered on him immediately as a face I had known somewhere, I was making no moves.

First I would have to remember who he was and where I had known him. I worked on my drink and I worked on my memory. Before I had come to the bottom of my drink, I had it. I took to congratulating myself on the wisdom of having made no moves. After all, it was no more than a face I had known and a man of whom I had known. We had never met. He could have no possible memory of me. It would have been striking up a new acquaintance, and it was clearly one I could never have wanted.

So I drank up and shook myself free of the joint. Sterling

remained in my mind only as a bit of an oddity. I could think of only one possible way that the man could have been back in the city. That would have been if he had been brought back to do some further singing. In that situation, however, he could hardly have been left loose to wander the town. He would have been kept securely tucked away. I couldn't imagine that he would have been permitted to wander unless hedged around with bodyguards. If anything was obvious, it was that the man had walked into the bar alone, naked to his enemies.

When I next saw Inspector Schmidt, I mentioned it to him. I was attaching no importance to it. I brought it up only as a curious sight around town. It could have been that I had seen a woman walk into Tiffany's accompanied by a python on a leash. It astonished me, therefore, when Schmitty pounced on it. For him it was obviously quite out of the python-on-a-leash category.

"You're sure?"

"I'd know that face anywhere."

"Did you speak to him?"

"Why would I speak to him? I never knew the man."

"There have been times you talked to strangers."

"He wasn't all that much a stranger. I knew who he was and what he was. Why would I want any part of him?"

"Something like doing your old buddy, Inspector Schmidt, a favor? How about that?"

"You? What's he to you? The man's never been charged with homicide. As I had it, he's never even been suspected of homicide, or is there something I don't know?"

"The man's an idiot. Coming back to town, wandering around loose. He's a sitting duck. So he does his drinking in a saloon where no man can hold a glass without sticking his pinky out. Okay. Maybe he won't be recognized there, but coming and going and anything else he can be doing in the city, he's a cinch to be spotted. In this town Jack Sterling has enemies like a stray mutt has fleas. Somebody's going to bump him off. So it would have been good if I could have gotten to him first."

"Crime prevention?" I asked.

"What's wrong with crime prevention?"

"But who'll want to knock him off now? He's sung his song. Isn't it too late?"

"For the babies he fingered it's never too late."

"Oh, come on, Schmitty! For them he's already done his worst. If they hit him now, they have everything to lose and nothing to gain."

"That's not the way they look at it."

"Revenge? At this late date revenge would be an expensive luxury. We're talking about businessmen. That their business ran the wrong side of the law is immaterial."

"That's right," Schmitty said. "They're businessmen, but they're far-seeing as well as practical."

"That's exactly what I've been saying."

"Not quite, really. You're ignoring their practical necessities."

"Like what?"

"Like keeping the troops in line. The guy talked. He wrecked the operation, and he got off scot-free. It's a bad precedent, and if they can help it, it's a precedent they won't let stand. If they are to have any future, they must get discipline established again. Nobody can talk and get away with it. The guy is going to pay sooner or later."

"And he doesn't know that?"

"He must know it. After all, he used to be in the business

himself. He knows the stuff they had him do to guys who showed even nothing more than some preliminary symptom of going loose lipped."

"Then that would be why he went to P.J.'s for his drinking, a place where he won't be recognized."

"You recognized him."

"I hardly count."

"The way you handled it, you can say that again."

"I meant I had no reason to go gunning for him," I said.

"The next time you see him in that dump . . ." Schmitty began.

I interrupted him. "I don't know when that will be," I said. "I don't stop in there all that often."

"But now you will," the inspector told me. "You're going to be one of their regulars. You're going to spend your evenings there."

"And?"

"First time you spot him again, you give me a buzz right away and then you start up a conversation with him. Make it real friendly. Keep him there till I can join you."

"What do I talk to him about? We swap memories of five years back?"

"I said hold him there. You don't want to scare him off."

"Okay. What do I say that doesn't scare him off?"

"What do you say when you get talking to a stranger in a bar?"

"Hello, beautiful. Can I buy you a drink?"

"It's not always that kind of stranger," Schmitty said.

"Weather. Politics. Mets. Knicks. Rangers. Yanks. Giants. Jets."

"That's it. Any of those or all of them. Get something started, and then you roll with it."

"And when you get there, what do you do?"

"Hand him back to his keepers. The Feds should be taking care of him. That was the deal. We have our precedents to think about too. A guy has been given protection. It's a bad precedent to let him get knocked off. The Feds handle it no better than this, and pretty soon there'll be nobody singing."

"So the problem belongs to the Feds," I said. "Why should I get into the act?"

"Crime prevention. I don't want him bumped off. I don't want anybody bumped off. It makes work for me, and I'm a lazy guy."

"That's no answer," I said.

It wasn't and Schmitty knew it wasn't. I suppose he'd been hoping I wouldn't press him on it. He squirmed a bit.

"No, it isn't," he said. "Anyone else, I could just put the word out on him. I'd have the whole force watching for him and between our guys and the Feds he'd be picked up pretty quick."

"And because it's Sterling?" I asked.

"Because it's Sterling, doing it that way I'd just be blowing the whistle on him. I'd be setting the wrong guys to be watching for him."

"You think there are men still in the department, men who slipped through five years ago?" I asked.

"Could be. When a thing is as big as that one was, that many people involved, you can hope you got all of them, but it's reasonably sure that you didn't. The chances are good that Sterling coughed up all the names he knew, and the chances are even better that he didn't know all the names. And that isn't all."

"What else?"

"Loyalties. The guys that got caught weren't without good friends on the force. Sterling's timing is lousy. Okay.

Not all of them have finished serving time. Not all are out on parole, but most of them are out. We've got cops who are clean and always have been, but they have friends who weren't."

"They'll tip these friends?"

"Right. More likely than not. Use your imagination. You know how it goes. Over a beer, just making talk. 'You know that Jack Sterling bastard. The word's out on him down at headquarters. The son-of-a-bitch is back in town.'"

"Inciting an old friend to murder?"

"He knows old buddy real well. He knows old buddy won't do anything about it. It's just interesting, something to talk about."

"And you're not ready to rely on his knowing old buddy well enough?"

"That's possible," the inspector said, "but what'd be certain is that the word is out. It'll get passed along. Overnight everybody knows, and everybody will include guys who will do something about it."

"So I'm elected to save Jack Sterling from his own stupidity," I said.

"I wish you would make the try," Schmitty said.

"And if I come out of it drinking nothing but white wine or Perrier with a twist?"

"Weaning you back to Bourbon won't be too hard. I'll buy the Virginia Gentleman and flatten your pinky."

"In that case," I said, "what have I got to lose?"

I should have known better. I had my evenings, and evenings spent in P.J.'s were going to be a dead loss. I gave it one evening and Sterling didn't show. I found myself listening in on some of the regulars. They were in hot discussion of a projected ad campaign. It was going to be for the promotion of perfumed toilet paper. It was going to be the biggest thing since jogging shoes.

I wondered how long the inspector would be keeping me at this imbecility. I could see no reason to believe that Sterling would ever hit that joint again. He could be going to a different P.J.'s every night. Doing it that way, he could go on for a long time before he would ever have to repeat. There was also no reason to think that he had come back to town for more than the quickest turnaround. Even when I'd mentioned him to Schmitty, he might already have pulled out.

I wasn't left to wonder for long. It was only the second evening and no more than a half hour into that when Inspector Schmidt took me off the hook. The bartender shouted my name. There was a call for Bagby. I knew it would have to be Schmitty. Nobody else knew I was there.

"If you've come down with any great new ideas," I said, "just don't tell me."

"You can pull out," the inspector said. "Of course, if you're having fun and want to stay . . ."

"I don't think he's going to show here again," I said.

"He's not showing anywhere again."

"You've got him?"

"Somebody got him. He's dead."

"Murdered?"

"Jack Sterlings don't die natural deaths, and they don't commit suicide."

"If I had buzzed you the other night?" I asked.

"If you had called me. If you could have held him. If I could have persuaded him for his own safety. Let's not overestimate ourselves. After all, I had nothing on which I could have pulled him in. He would have had to cooperate for his own good."

"That's not the way you were talking before," I said.

"I was talking about what I hoped I maybe could do," Schmitty said. "There was never any guarantee. I was building it up to get you to work on it with me. Relax, Baggy. You're not to blame. We can't win them all, and anyhow the big if was if he'd had the sense to stay where he was and not break his cover. Coming back here, that was suicidal."

"Who did it?" I asked.

"That's what I have to find out."

"Any ideas?"

"Too many. Too many likely candidates."

"Then it'll be a roundup and checking alibis?"

"Without expecting much out of that," the inspector said. "Too many of the birds who wanted him dead don't do that kind of work for themselves. They put out contracts. That's routine and we'll run it through, but I'm not looking for it to give us much."

"Then what?"

"What brought him back? Who brought him back? If I can get those answers," Schmitty said.

"Makings of a story," I said.

"It could be the one you'll call 'Inspector Schmidt Falls on His Face.'"

"Then I better get on it with you," I said. "That would be something that shouldn't be missed."

# CHAPTER 2

"Then come on over," the inspector said. "It's only a hop and a jump. You had him for a neighbor."

"Where?"

He gave me the address and it was as he said, only a few doors up the avenue. I knew those houses along the avenue. They had been tenements, but not the cold-water flats with the shared toilets out in the hall. These had been built as accommodations several cuts above that. They'd had heat and hot water and all the requisite plumbing inside the boundaries of each flat.

Most of them had been converted for stores at street level with the upper stories modernized and fancied up. The modernization consisted of air-conditioning, slicked up bathrooms, and modern kitchens. They were still walkups, and the mice and the roaches were solidly established in the old walls. None of the surface modernization could eliminate them.

Since they were in what was considered a good part of town, those flats had for a considerable time been renting at figures I could never make myself believe. In giving me the address, the inspector had told me that it was the third-floor-rear.

As I was pulling out of the bar, I was telling myself that it would have to be one of the buildings that hadn't been put through the modernization process even though I'd heard that rentals in even those defied belief. It seemed to me that if Sterling had been paying anything of that order for the roof over his head, he must have been doing very well. I was also trying to recall whether there was a house in that block that hadn't been slicked up. I couldn't remember any.

I've checked since. There aren't any unmodified jobs in the whole row, but the house at the address the inspector had given me was easily the most fancied up of the lot. It was the one where the street-level store was the unisex barber shop, all black and silver and *art nouveau* calculated to make a shampoo and trim feel like attendance at a Black Mass. Every barber in the place was blown dry to an extent to which no customer could ever aspire. The aim appeared to be to make it seem as though human scalps sprouted cotton candy.

You'd have to know the way these building conversions have been done. At street level there is the storefront and alongside it a narrow door that leads to a pocket of vestibule with a narrow hall and a narrow staircase beyond. That staircase is the only access to the apartments up above. There is no back stairway and no service entrance.

A cab was pulled up at the curb in front of the building and a woman was lifting a small suitcase into it and simultaneously arguing with the cabbie. It was a heated argument. The cabbie was shouting. The woman was more restrained—at least she was holding the volume of her voice down. In intensity it was more than a match for the cabbie's.

"This is the address you guv me, lady," the cabbie was saying.

"Don't be ridiculous. Does this look like the kind of place I'd be going to?"

"I don't know what kind of places you go to, lady."

"If you don't know, then shut up. I do know and this is not the place."

"It's where you told me."

By that time she was in the cab, but the windows were down. I could still hear them.

"Oh, shut up and get going."

"Get going where?"

"Just get going. I'll tell you where."

The cabbie pulled away from the curb and I headed into the little vestibule. In the inner hall at the foot of the stairs the inevitable cop was stationed. Since he was a precinct man and this was my home precinct, he knew me and was aware of my association with Inspector Schmidt.

"The inspector's upstairs," he said. "Third-floor-rear. I don't know if you want to go up, Mr. Bagby, but anyway brace yourself. It's a smeller."

I could do without that kind, and who couldn't? It set me off, however, on some simple arithmetic. It was no more than forty-eight hours since I had seen the man alive, and this was news that narrowed the margins. Deterioration, of course, begins at the moment of death if not before, but it is not so rapid that it will assail the nose within a matter of hours. That takes days. In a warm room the process will be accelerated, but I did have my own measurement of the time. It had to be something less than forty-eight hours. Even under conditions conducive to the greatest acceleration it couldn't have been much less than the forty-eight hours. Jack Sterling, therefore, had been killed shortly after I had seen him. I was reading it for almost immediately after, certainly no later than that same evening.

The third-floor-rear was a two-room-kitchenette-and-bath job. The living room showed all the trappings of the good life as it is lived by the affluent inhabitants of these apartments that have been elevated into the luxury class. The pile of the carpeting didn't tickle my ankles, but that was only because I am not flat-footed.

The furniture had that elegant austerity that suggests a private clinic run for people who like their comfort and are prepared to pay for it. It was all lovingly finished blond woods and impeccably fashioned chrome. There was a bar. It was chrome framed and glass fronted.

It had to be glass because otherwise one couldn't have seen the labels on the bottles shelved behind that bar front. The vodka was Polish. The Scotch was one of the straight malt whiskies. The cognac was the thirty-year-old, and the armagnac was as venerable. It was a setting of ostentatiously expensive simplicity.

The bedroom was more of the same, but there I was diverted from taking much notice of the decor. There was the smell. That cop downstairs hadn't exaggerated. Jack Sterling was not newly dead. The body was lying face down on the big bed. It was totally naked, and there was no need to ask how he had been killed. The knife planted in his back answered for that. There was some blood. I could see where a trickle from the wound had dried on the body. On the black satin sheets the bloodstains showed up only as dull areas where the staining had robbed the satin of its light-reflecting sheen.

Despite all the inspector had just been saying about how very thin the possibility of forestalling this killing had always been, on the way up the avenue I had been plagued by the thought that I could have done it. Even after I'd had the word from the patrolman down in the hall, I'd been thinking that if on my own I had followed the procedure Schmitty had later set up for me—if I had called the inspector and if I had held Sterling in conversation till the inspector could have made it over to P.J.'s and taken over—we might have been in time.

He would have had to listen to Inspector Schmidt. He would have had to put himself under police protection and to have agreed to being again spirited out of town without so much as going back to the apartment. It had come to seem a proposition riddled with ifs, but I couldn't shed the thought that we might just have pulled it off.

Seeing the body and that bedroom's accompanying evidence lifted even that small load off me. A couple of streaks lightly encrusted with blood crisscrossed the corpse's buttocks and on the black satin sheet alongside the body lay the small whip.

"Sex crime," I said. I can't always refrain from remarking on the obvious.

"Looks like it, doesn't it?" the inspector said.

"What else? Certainly it isn't likely that you could have dissuaded him from exposing himself to this."

"If it wasn't that it was Jack Sterling," Schmitty said, "there'd be no reason for not settling for the obvious."

"I know that there are plenty who don't look the part, but he did. He may not have had the mannerisms, but he had the look."

The inspector agreed but only within limits. "We saw it," he said, "and we could speculate about it. Now, of course, the speculations are confirmed. His one-time colleagues knew him better than we ever could. What's to say they wouldn't have known the best way to get at him? They put on to him a guy he'll be certain to turn his back on, and they have him rubbed out under circumstances that will scream sex crime. Isn't that the greatest? The dumb cops will never think to go looking past that."

It wasn't like Inspector Schmidt to get his feet so deeply mired in a hypothesis that he couldn't walk away from it any time the evidence wiped it out.

"Aren't you reaching, Schmitty?" I asked.

The question brought me what I should have expected. I have been exposed to his way of thinking for far too many years not to know that a major instrument in his arsenal of logic has always been Occam's Razor. Until that time many years ago when he first threw it at me and I put the name to it and told him about William Occam, he had never heard of the good friar or of his contributions to philosophical reasoning. He had, nevertheless, in his operations always adhered to the principle. When confronted with two possible hypotheses, explore the simpler one.

"Jack Sterling comes back into the territory where he's marked for murder. He sticks his neck out."

"In this case it looks as though it was the other end he stuck out," I said.

"Both ends. So the people who are gunning for him are relieved of the job of knocking him off?"

"It could happen. It's masochism's built-in risk."

"It's too much the lucky coincidence. I can't trust it. Also the scene is too neatly set. It's got a strong smell of camouflage."

"The smell is real enough," I said, "and as it strikes me, the scene is too."

"The guy's dead. That much of it is real. I need confirmation from the Medical Examiner before I can believe the rest of it. Even then I don't think I'll believe it."

"Apart from the coincidence aspect," I asked, "what can't you believe?"

"Sex crime."

We pulled out of there, leaving the body and the bedroom to the technicians. The inspector in due time would
have full reports from them. As much as was visible to the
naked eye we had seen. It looked as though nothing in the
room had been disturbed. There was not even the slightest
sign of a struggle. On the testimony of the contents of the
closets and of the bathroom medicine cabinet, Jack Sterling had not been occupying the premises alone. Along
with what could have been taken to be his stuff, the closets
also had hanging in them an array of women's clothes. The
medicine cabinet was furnished with two distinct sets of
cosmetics—his and hers. There was deodorant, after-shave,
talcum, toilet water, and perfume all in one of those scents
gargantuan line-backers tout on TV as the secret of their
masculinity. That was one shelf. On another was lipstick,
eyeshadow, face powder, something called a blusher (I
think it used to be called rouge), dusting powder, deodorant, and perfume all of a fragrance that one Gabor or
another guarantees as an infallible man catcher.

"Any line on his cohabitant?" I asked when we were on
the way down the stairs.

"Not yet," Schmitty said, "if he had one."

"The clothes," I said. "The rest of the female stuff."

"The clothes," Schmitty told me, "would fit a big dame.
They even look as though they would fit a dame who was
Sterling's size."

"Transvestite? Sterling?"

"Hey, Baggy! Since when have you been so hooked on
sex?"

"You suggested the idea, Inspector Schmidt. So what
would you call it?"

"What about disguise? It was open season on Jack Sterling and he knew it. So when he left the game preserve where he had been protected, isn't it possible that he would have been taking steps?"

"Possible," I said, "but then why wasn't he in disguise the night I saw him?"

"Which was also the night he got the knife in his back," Schmitty said. "That night he might have dressed for what he was looking for."

"On the other hand, he wouldn't be the first guy to swing both ways," I said.

"Exactly," the inspector agreed. "On that point we keep our thinking open until we learn more. But I can't see a sex murder that's anything less than a climax act," he said. "There's rape that ends in murder because the victim must be silenced. This wasn't rape. We can rule that out. There would be some indication of struggle. That leaves us stuck with the climax act, and from the look of the body the knife came into play at a stage of early preliminary."

That seemed clear enough. A man who knew Sterling's proclivities could have gone into a little sex play, just enough to put his victim in convenient position for the knife in his back. Obviously it couldn't have been anyone that Sterling knew would be out to knock him off. He would never have offered his back to any of that crowd, but it could have been a stranger, a hired killer who had been well briefed by someone who knew. There was still one point where I was stuck.

"You said that if you did get the evidence from the ME, even that wouldn't clinch it."

"It wouldn't," the inspector said, "because we'd still have the possibility that the man had been out to bump Sterling off but he allowed himself the luxury of letting it wait until he'd had his fun first."

Although we had pulled out of the apartment, we hadn't gone far, just at a remove sufficient to take us away from the smell. We were doing our talking on the stairs and during a cigarette pause on the street in front of the building. Schmitty bit it off by tossing away his cigarette and heading into the barber shop.

I followed after him. Neither attendants nor patrons showed any interest in us. Neither of us had the right look. We could, of course, have been in there to have ourselves restyled, but if any of the hairdressers had considered that possibility, he would, I was guessing, have dismissed us as material on which he could work none of his peculiar artistry.

The inspector approached the lad who was working the nearest chair.

"I'm looking for Jack," he said.

"You must mean Jacques."

"Jack—Jacques. Where is he?"

"He's not well."

"I know that, but where has he gone to be not well?"

"He wouldn't want to see anyone now. You'll have to come back."

"He'll see us." Schmitty produced his ID.

"About upstairs?" the hairdresser asked.

"That's it. How could you ever guess?"

"He's in the back room." Turning to the man whose beard he'd been dyeing, he began making his excuses. When he saw us heading for the back room he had indicated, he cut them short. "Hey," he said, scampering after us. "You can't just go in there. I'll go and see if he's all right."

"You left your customer half done or does the gentleman

want the tortoiseshell look?" the inspector said. "Jack will be right enough for us."

We went on into the back room, leaving the hairdresser to mutter to himself. If the shop was fancy, the back room was fancier. This would be where the patrons went to change into the black-and-silver smocks. Any restraint that might have been operative in the decoration of the shop had here been thrown to the winds. The room looked like a bargain-basement seraglio. There was a sofa so excessively tufted that it looked as though it had made an unsuccessful recovery from smallpox. The upholstery was sickly green and, reclining on it, Jacques could have been a chameleon disappearing into his background. His face had assumed the color of the upholstery.

A neatly folded towel soaked in cologne covered his forehead and his eyes. The room was stuffy—nothing there to breathe but the cologne. Hearing us come in, he lifted the towel just enough to reveal one bleary eye and that only briefly. With great care he repositioned the towel before he spoke.

"Inspector," he said. "I've been spitting up my guts. If I so much as move, I'll be doing it again."

"Don't move," Schmitty said. "I just have a few questions."

"Can't they wait?"

"They can't. You're only sick, mister. That guy upstairs is dead."

Jacques moaned. The inspector persisted.

"You said upstairs that you were the one who found him," he said.

"And I wish I hadn't. I'm going to have nightmares the rest of my life."

"You'll forget it."

"I won't, not ever. I'm sensitive, Inspector. You can never imagine how sensitive."

Talking about himself and his sensitivity seemed to have something of a restorative effect on the man. His color improved. He removed the towel. He even sat up.

"You went up there and you found him. How did you come to go up there?"

"Oh, that was Rudy."

"Who's Rudy?"

"Rudy is my porter. I have him working in the atelier. He keeps it tidy. He sweeps up the hair, mops up spills, all that. After we close he stays on to clean."

"That's down here. I want to know about upstairs."

"A couple of times a week he comes in early, and before we open up he goes up and cleans for her."

"Who's her?"

"Miss Smith."

"Who's Miss Smith?"

"It's her apartment."

"Third-floor-rear?"

"That's where you want to know about, isn't it?"

"It is. Just Miss Smith? No more name than that?"

"Mary Smith."

Inspector Schmidt looked skeptical. Jacques caught the look.

"There are Smiths," he said. "There are Mary Smiths—lots of them."

"And not all of them are real Mary Smiths."

Jacques shrugged. "I wouldn't know about that. She's Mary Smith on the lease, and her bank reference was Mary Smith. Her rent checks are signed Mary Smith and they don't bounce."

"Okay. She's your tenant. The guy upstairs? Where does he come in?"

"He's been in the apartment about a week." Jacques broke off for a moment or two of thought. With the index finger of his right hand, he ticked off the glossily manicured fingers of his left. He was evidently counting days. With a nod of satisfaction he spoke again. "Yes," he said. "It was just a week ago."

"Just a week ago Mary Smith brought him here to stay?"

"She came home. She had been away for about a month. She's away more than she ever is here. She uses the apartment only as a *pied-à-terre*. This time he was with her. She stayed only the one night, and then she was off again with him staying on in the apartment alone after that."

I started to speak. The attempt drew me a scowl from the inspector. He wanted no interruptions. Ordinarily I would have held it, but I felt that, if anything, he was going to want to know why I hadn't told him sooner.

"Inspector," I said. "There's something I think you should know. If you'll give me just a moment . . ."

He didn't like it, but he pulled me aside. I could tell that he was expecting nothing, but he'd decided it would be the only way he could get me off his back.

I handled it with a quick whisper, filling him in on the dame and her argument with the cab driver. He erased the scowl.

"She'd seen the precinct guy I've got in the vestibule," he said.

"I don't see how she could have missed."

"He's a big hunk of cop," Schmitty said. "Not easily overlooked."

Returning to Jacques, he set off on another line of ques-

tioning. "Your Mary Smith," he said, "what does she look
like?"

"She's tall," Jacques said. "Tall for a woman and she's
big—not fat big but big. She's always beautifully groomed
and she knows how to dress—beautiful clothes, excellent
taste, and always the things that are just right for her.
Women her size have to be very knowing about clothes.
They must have faultless taste and a sure sense of what is
right for them. The smallest misjudgment and they look
freakish. So many big women make the mistake of trying
to dress in a way they think will minimize their size. She
dresses in a way that makes the most of her size. The effect
is handsome and arresting."

While he was speaking, Schmitty was looking to me. I
was nodding. I might have been less professional in my description of the woman I'd seen, but there was nothing in
what Jacques was saying that didn't fit. The inspector,
however, was getting more than he needed of the fashion
approach.

"Hair color?" he asked.

"Brown, very subtle henna," Jacques said. "I can have
no quarrel with the way the color is handled, but she could
do better than that close-cropped-cap effect. I've always
wished we could restyle her. We could do something quite
remarkable for her, but it's never been any good my pushing it. She's away so much of the time that more times than
not it would be in someone else's hands and it would be
ruined. It's regrettable, but I must admit that she is wise to
keep it as she does. After all, it is a style anyone can handle."

Again the inspector was getting more than he could possibly have wanted. He had looked to me and I had given him
my nod to the subtly henna close-cropped cap.

"She brought him here and she was here with him only the one night before she took off again. Did she tell you how long she would be gone this time?"

"No, but then she never has. She just comes and goes. When she is away at the first of the month, I always have her check in the mail. She's never behind on the rent, not by even so much as a day."

"Mailed from where?"

"From where?" Jacques looked startled. "I'm sure I don't know."

"Never noticed the postmarks?"

"Why would I notice postmarks?"

"Curiosity. Interest in a tenant."

Jacques shrugged. It might have been that he was trying to indicate that postmarks bored him. Schmitty didn't push it.

"The guy upstairs? What was his name?"

"I haven't the faintest idea. We were never introduced."

"I thought she might have told you that she was going off and that Mr. Soandso would be using the apartment during her absence."

Jacques shook his head.

"She just brought him in and then went away leaving him in possession? No explanation to you and no questions asked?"

"She had no reason to explain, and I had no reason to question. It's her apartment. She pays the rent. If she had a man up there with her, that was her business. They were quiet. Should I have gone prying into her private life?"

"It was her apartment, but she went away, turning it over to a man you knew nothing about. You hadn't seen any references from him, had you?"

"It wasn't a sublet. If she chose to give someone the use

of the apartment while she was away . . ." Jacques gave it another of his shrugs.

"So you were happy about the whole thing?"

"Not exactly happy, Inspector."

"You had misgivings. Tell me about them."

"It was Rudy."

"Oh, yes, Rudy. Rudy goes up there to clean. He reported something that made you unhappy?"

"She left in the morning early. That same morning after she'd gone Rudy went up there to do her apartment. It was one of his regular days; he has a key and he just goes up there and lets himself in. Rudy never rings the bell—he just goes in and cleans. He went up that morning not knowing the man would be there, but the man was there, and when Rudy went in, the man met him with a gun. I can tell you. It terrified Rudy."

"He was just terrified," Schmitty said. "He wasn't shot?"

"No, as he tells it . . ." Jacques began.

The inspector interrupted. "Is Rudy out front now?"

"Yes, he is."

"Call him back here. I'd like him to tell it."

"He has his work to do."

"And I have mine," Schmitty said. "Get him in here."

# CHAPTER 3

Rudy came carrying his floor brush and pan. The brush
was black and the pan was silver. Only the hair sweepings
in the pan marred the effect. They were faintly pink.

"Inspector Schmidt wants to know about the man in
Miss Smith's apartment," Jacques said.

"He was a crazy," Rudy said.

"You have a key to the apartment."

The inspector was prompting the man.

"I had a key. The crazy took it away from me."

Rudy was a willing witness, but he could hardly have
been more lacking in the art of narrative. The step-by-step
detailed account that the inspector wanted from him took
much extracting. In essence his story was simple enough.
As Jacques had already told us, Rudy had gone up to the
apartment loaded down with his cleaning gear. He had
unlocked the door and was pushing it open with his foot
while he had both hands busy gathering up the mops and
brushes and pails he had set down while he worked the
key.

Straightening up with all that stuff in his hands, he'd
found himself confronted with the gun. In panic he
dropped everything. Sterling, however, presumably recog-
nizing him as the porter, lowered the gun; but he stood
fast, barring Rudy from the apartment.

"He asked me what I wanted. I told him it was my day

to clean. He said he didn't want the place cleaned. He didn't want me coming up there. He didn't want nobody coming up there. He made me give him the key. He didn't want nobody walking in on him with no keys. He said he would clean the place himself. He said I was to stay away from there if I knew what was good for me."

"Anything else?" Schmitty asked.

"What else? I wasn't waiting for nothing else. I gave him the key and I got back downstairs quick. I told Mr. Jacques."

The inspector turned to Jacques. "And you weren't entirely happy?" he said.

"A gun? Who's happy with a gun, Inspector?"

"But you did nothing about it?"

"What could I do about it? It would have to wait until Miss Smith would be back. I was going to take it up with her."

"You went up there tonight because of Rudy."

"Partly because of Rudy. Rudy has been fussing ever since that morning. He's been worrying that Miss Smith will come back and find that he hasn't been up there to clean and he'll lose the job. The days he should have been up there and hasn't been are days' pay he's been losing. He kept saying that maybe the man wasn't up there anymore. It had been a couple of days since he'd last seen him come in or go out."

The inspector took it back to Rudy. "You watched his comings and goings?" he asked.

"After I seen him the last time. That started me up watching."

"And you haven't seen him since?"

"No. Not since the last time."

"When was that?"

"Two days back. The night before last. I'd just finished here and I locked up. I was out in the street. I was going home."

"You saw him in the street?"

"I seen him going in. He was bringing a dame in with him."

"Miss Smith?"

"No, not her. A bimbo, a real bimbo. Cheap red wig and one of them dresses, it's tight on the ass. She had such a big ass that maybe any dress would be tight on it."

He held out his hands to suggest the span of the rear elevation. Considerable allowance had to be made for exaggeration. He was indicating something well out of the human range.

Although less explicit and less knowing in such matters, Rudy, like his employer, was unstinting in his admiration of the grooming and the dress of the tenant who held the lease on the third-floor-rear. Miss Smith was a lady. She dressed like a lady and she looked like a lady.

"Whores," he said. "We got them on the street over this side of town too, but not like that one. One of that kind he had to bring over from Eigth Avenue."

He was, of course, referring to that stretch of Eighth Avenue that has been called the Minnesota Strip. The name derives from the fresh-faced teenage blondes who have run away from their midwestern homes and, picked up by pimps, have been set to patrolling the area. Schmitty pounced on it. He's Homicide and not Vice Squad, but he knows his city.

"A big, overgrown kid?" he asked.

"No kid," Rudy said. "They don't get so they look like that one without they been out on the street for years."

Schmitty worked on it some more, but at length he was

convinced that Rudy had no more to give him. He turned back to Jacques.

"You still haven't told me why you went up there to-night," he said.

"A lot of reasons," Jacques said. "Rudy kept nagging me. I didn't like it that the apartment wasn't being cleaned and that he hadn't been putting out any garbage. In these old houses you can't keep it nice unless you work at it all the time. Let one apartment go neglected for a week or more and first thing you know you've got roach trouble. They get started in one apartment and then they're all over the building. I live here myself—I have the whole second floor. I had to go up there."

"Even though you had a man up there who met visitors with a gun and who didn't want people having a key to the place? You went up and let yourself in?"

"Yes, Rudy had told me that the man had taken his key and that he said he didn't want anyone having a key, but he wasn't the tenant and it is my property. I have to have a key, particularly to her apartment. With most of the time nobody up there, I have to be able to get in. There can be a leak; there can be a fire."

"I understand that, but didn't you think you'd be going up there to face a gun?"

Torn between two worries, concern for his property and concern for his skin, Jacques had gone up to the third-floor-rear but not without taking all possible precautions.

"I wasn't about to use my key and just walk in on him," he said. "In the first place there was the gun, but I also thought it would be better if he didn't know I had a key. I figured he'd want to take it away from me, and I wasn't about to argue with a gun."

He had gone upstairs and rung the bell. He had done a

lot of ringing, pressing the bell and waiting, trying again and again until he was convinced that there could be nobody in the apartment. It was only then that he'd brought out his key. He went in and found the body.

"Did you touch anything?"

"Touch anything?" The question outraged him. "I was sick. I was too sick to touch anything. It was all I could do to get myself out of there and come back down here. Even so, I was sick on the stairs. I was so sick I couldn't even call the police. One of my men made the call for me."

That was the whole of what was to be had out of Jacques and Rudy. We went the few steps down the avenue to P.J.'s. Things there seemed to be much as they had been an hour and more earlier when the inspector's call had pulled me out of that scene of subdued merriment. The white-wine drinkers were there in force. The people who were debauching themselves with the Perrier and a twist were sinking deeper and deeper into the depravity of their low habit.

We bellied up to the bar and Schmitty fell into the spirit of the place. He ordered himself Perrier and a twist. Inspector Schmidt doesn't drink on duty, and here he had an opportunity to do his not drinking within the accepted customs of the establishment. Since my involvement was only semi-official if even that, I spoke for what I needed—Bourbon with a beer chaser. Although I had done far better than Jacques in standing up to the third-floor-rear, the smell was still with me. I needed strong medicine.

Inspector Schmidt identified himself. The bartender reacted with no show of interest. If you know bartenders, you may be thinking that was uncharacteristic, but this bartender was no true member of the breed. He had the look—the beefy, red face; the thick neck; the water-slicked hair; the big, red hands; white shirt; green bow-tie, even green sleeve garters—but it had always seemed to me that at heart he was a cocktail-lounger dressed for the saloon part.

He asked the suitable question, but it was languid. "Anything I can do for you, Inspector?"

"You had a woman in here two nights ago. She picked up a customer and they left together."

"You've got the wrong spot, Inspector. We're not that kind of a joint."

"It can happen anywhere," Schmitty said.

The bartender wiped his bar. It made no difference that the bar hadn't needed wiping. It was a bartender sort of thing to do. It was not inevitably a play for time. It could have been no more than a part of the act like the bow-tie and the sleeve garters. Schmitty waited.

"Sure." The bartender had found his answer. "Sure, but how can a guy police it? You have a dame who comes in all the time. Night after night you can see she's working the joint. She leaves with a guy once. The next night she leaves with another guy, and the night after still another guy. That way you know what makes. It don't just happen every time she comes in here she runs on some guy she's known from way back. She's cruising and no mistake. So, okay. That way you know. You give her the heave-ho and you let her know you ain't holding still for her coming back. It's like that, you can handle it, but I ain't ever had the problem here."

It was a long speech, far too long, well up into the dimensions of protesting too much.

"Relax, brother," Schmitty said. "I'm not Vice Squad. I'm Homicide."

The inspector had been in the business too long to have the delusion that Homicide could be a relaxing word. For his purposes that barkeep could have been tense to the point of breaking. He just wanted the man more usefully oriented.

"Homicide?" the man asked. "That thing up the avenue?"

"What thing up the avenue?"

"You tell me, Inspector. I just been seeing the police cars and like that. I been figuring a burglary."

"You lost a customer."

"The dame you think was in here?"

"The man she left with."

"A guy got knocked off and a dame done it?"

"Somebody done it."

Inspector Schmidt has found that questioning is likely to go better if he talks to people in their own language.

There was a customer at the bar. Through all of this he had been edging closer and closer. He was all ears. At this point, however, he became mouth as well.

"Two nights back, Paddy," he said. "The big redhead with the granite jaw and the satin *derrière*. I was wondering where she'd strayed from."

Paddy knitted his brows. He was going through the motions of taking deep soundings into his memory.

"Big redhead," he mumbled.

The customer tried to come to his assistance.

"There was this strange chap," he said. "Nobody knew him, but he was beginning to be like one of the regulars. He'd been coming in every night for—I don't know—I guess three or four nights. He'd sit around and drink alone."

Paddy shook himself. He was going through the act of having made his best effort to recall and now he was giving up on it.

"It must be I was too busy tending bar to take any notice," he said.

It was feeble. Bartenders have great peripheral vision. What a bartender fails to notice is just not there to be seen. That goes for the cocktail-lounge types as well. In that respect they are no different from the real thing.

The customer wasn't satisfied. He leaned forward over the bar, looking past the inspector to focus on me.

"You were here that night," he said. "I remember you. You saw this chap. You were wondering about him like everyone else, but you were letting it show."

"I watch everybody," I said. "It's a habit. What did the guy look like?"

"Ever been to Paris?"

"What's Paris got to do with it?" the inspector asked.

"Nothing, but I was asking your friend."

"I've been to Paris," I said.

"The Louvre?"

"Even the Louvre."

Schmitty was having no patience with this. I felt him stirring beside me. I nudged him. I had a hunch we were getting somewhere. He gave me a look, but he subsided and let it ride along.

"If you know the Leonardo St. John," the man said. "Sweet, soft face, even a touch overripe."

I had been thinking of a saint out of a Mannerist painting, but this was close enough. The Mannerists did derive from Leonardo.

"That guy," I said. "Yes, I remember. You don't often see a face like that."

"If you remember him," the man said, "you can't have forgotten the woman."

"You do make her sound memorable," I said. "She must have turned up after I took off."

Inspector Schmidt climbed back onto it and directed it at Paddy.

"Everybody else remembers," he said, "and you don't?"

"Yes and no," Paddy said.

"What does that mean? How much yes and how much no?"

"I'm beginning to remember the guy. I remember one of those nights he was coming in. Mr. Froman, here, he said the guy looked like Saint John. Anyway he hasn't been around the last couple of days."

"He's been dead the last couple of days," the inspector said. "He was last seen going into his place with the big redhead, and that was two nights ago."

Froman whistled. "She was one tough-looking babe," he said. "She looked tough enough for anything. Did she kill him?"

"She was with him when he was last seen," Schmitty said. "And he's been dead long enough for it to have happened that same night."

Froman shuddered. "You never know," he said.

"You come in here regularly, Mr. Froman?" Schmitty asked.

"It's my home away from home. If Paddy didn't see me here across the bar, he'd think he hadn't opened up."

"If you're here every night and your memory is so much better than Paddy's, perhaps you can tell me. The woman? Had you ever seen her here before?"

"The satin-sheathed Amazon? No. That one evening she just strayed in out of the night and she lost no time about getting down to business. She looked us all over, made her choice, and went right about cutting Saint John out of the herd. If you ask me, he wasn't hard to get. The way he took to her, you could think they were made for each other."

"Would you say they struck up an acquaintance here? They hadn't known each other before?"

"No question about it. It was quick and raw and obvious. She just barged up to him and made her bid. I even heard what she said."

"What did she say?"

Froman snickered. "This you won't believe, but I can give it to you word for word."

"That," the inspector said, "I would like."

" 'Hello, handsome. You look lonely.' Can you believe it? But I swear."

"What did he say?"

" 'Can I buy you a drink?' "

"Then what?"

Froman laughed. He turned to Paddy.

"Now this," he said, "you can't have forgotten. Believe it or not, she asked for sauterne and 7-Up. Paddy, you can't have forgotten sauterne and 7-Up."

"Women ask for it," Paddy said. "You just ain't never tended bar, Mr. Froman."

Inspector Schmidt pushed back into it.

"Then what?" he said. "Did you hear any more?"

"No. They took their drinks and went to one of the booths in the back. They were back there and it looked as though they were whispering. It also looked as though they might have been grabbing feels. They drank up and left together. It was a great show. You don't often see one like that."

The inspector turned to Paddy. I wish I could reproduce his commiserating tone.

"And you missed the whole thing," he said.

Froman jumped back into it. "He was busy," he said. "Somehow or other that was a big night. I've never seen the place so jammed. How Paddy was keeping up with all the orders I'll never know."

It seemed to me that this was our night for people who protested too much.

"The place was jammed," Schmitty said, "but when those two looked for a place to be alone, they had no trouble finding an empty booth."

"Them booths in the back," Paddy said. "They're always going to waste. People like to hang up front where the action is."

"Mr. Froman found the action in that booth in back."

"They fascinated me," Froman said. "I had the leisure to observe them. Paddy didn't."

After having worked so hard at jogging Paddy's memory, he was now doing a turnabout to help the barman with his cover-up. I wasn't finding that too strange. The man was in his favorite haunt. Being on good terms with the bartender would be part of what made the place for him. He had opened his big mouth and, even though he had been carried away by the droll story, and, immersed in being the life of the party had been slow to notice that he was not pleasing Paddy, he had now at long last wakened to the situation and was doing his best to make amends. Any fool would know that in conversation with the police there would never be a barkeep who would not be eager to push the thought that he ran a nice, clean place where he permitted no hanky-panky.

The inspector made a note of Froman's full name. It was

Christopher Froman, and his address had him living directly across the street from me. It's a big apartment house over there. He also furnished his telephone number. The inspector need only call him and he would be at the inspector's service. Schmitty indicated that he might want him to look at some pictures.

"You might be able to help us find the redhead," Schmitty said. "I want to talk to her."

"I'll know her anywhere," Froman said. "If I see her around, can I call you?"

Schmitty gave him a number. He also suggested that, since Froman and I were neighbors, Froman could just cross the street and get the word to me.

By the time we pulled out of P.J.'s the atelier had closed for the night. It was dark. Since the meat wagon that had been standing out front was no longer there, it could be as-sumed that the body had been removed. Where the meat wagon had been standing there was now a cab at the curb. The cop who had been posted in the vestibule was now out front. He was talking to a man. We sauntered the few yards and joined them.

"Funniest fare I ever had," the man was saying, "and I've had them funny."

"Tell me," Schmitty said.

"Tell you what, mister?"

The man was in conversation with a friendly cop. He was welcoming no intrusions. The precinct man took care of that. He identified the inspector.

"Geez," the man said. "Excuse me, Inspector. I didn't know."

"That your cab?" Schmitty asked.

The cabbie started toward it. "I'll pull it right out of there, Inspector. I just stopped a moment to ask."

"Leave it," Schmitty said. "It's all right where it is. You stopped to ask what?"

"What happened here. I had this dame, craziest fare I ever had."

"Tell me about her."

"I picked her up at the East Side Air Terminal. She gives me this address. I bring her here. She pays me off. No argument, even a good tip. I unload her bag for her. She gets out of the cab and picks up her bag and then, bang, she turns around and she says this ain't where she wanted to go. What did I take her here for? I tell her it's the address she give me. She loads her bag back into the cab and tells me to take her away from here."

"Just away from here? No new address?"

"She didn't have no new address. It was this address she guv me, and now she's saying it ain't the place. She's saying I'm dumb. I got it wrong. I'm trying to be patient with her. You know. The customer is always right even when they ain't."

"Then where did she have you take her?"

"No place."

"Come on! You dropped her somewhere. You haven't still got her in your cab."

"Yeah. She keeps telling me how it's the right address but this ain't the right place, like maybe I don't know Third Avenue from Fifth and like I can't read house numbers."

"Okay. Where did you take her then?"

"I told her I couldn't do any better for this address. It was here and it wasn't nowhere else. So like I'm crazy and she ain't, she tells me to take her back. She'll find a cabbie at the air terminal, another cabbie, one what knows his way around. I wanted to just pull up and throw her out of the cab."

"But you didn't."

The cabbie laughed. It was a laugh that spoke more for embarrassment than for mirth.

"I knowed better than to even try," he said. "That was one big dame, one helluva lot bigger than me. I wasn't about to go tangling with her. They all got fingernails, but fingernails and muscles too, Inspector?"

"So you took her back to the air terminal?"

"Yeah."

"She switched to another cab?"

"No, she didn't."

"How do you know she didn't?"

"I hung on there and watched. Crazy like that, I was itching to know."

He had expected that at the terminal she would have just headed for the cab rank and he would see the cab she took. He would pick up the license number and he'd know the cabbie.

"All us guys, we work that cab rank down there at the air terminal, we know each other."

He couldn't imagine what she would do in another cab and he was curious. Was she going to give another driver this same address and end up with this same argument? So he was watching. She took her bag. She paid him off again and she tipped him again.

"That was funny, too," he said. "The clock was just the same. Air terminal to here and here to air terminal. It was the same distance and we hit about the same amount of traffic. So on this second fare her tip is bigger, twice what she guv me the first time. I guess it was because she knew she'd been giving me a bad time. She wasn't going to apologize or like that, but . . ."

"Then what did she do?"

"She went back into the air terminal."

"And stayed in there till you had taken off?"

"I don't know, Inspector. She went in and after she didn't come out again, I left the cab parked and I went inside to look around. The terminal, ain't like any of them terminals out at the airport. It ain't so big. You can find people. She wasn't anywhere in there unless maybe she was in the john. I thought of that and I hung around waiting for maybe she'd come out, but she didn't come out and I wasn't making no money that way. I didn't have the whole night. But I can tell you this: If she was in the john, she was in there a lot longer than even the slowest dame ever takes."

He'd returned to his cab and picked up a fare. He had been hacking ever since.

"The fare I had just now," he said, "it was to just a few blocks down the avenue. I was so close and I got to thinking that maybe I read the house number wrong or something. I was going by. So I stopped and looked. I hadn't gotten it wrong. Then I seen all them cops coming out like something maybe happened here. So I asked."

Inspector Schmidt tried for the cabbie's description of his strange fare. The man didn't have even Rudy's degree of expertise in the areas of female grooming and women's clothes, but he did better than just big and muscles and fingernails. What he was able to offer tallied well enough with the descriptions we'd had of Mary Smith and with my memory of the woman I'd seen. That I had expected. There could hardly have been two of them.

"She looked like she was loaded," he said, finishing his description. "Expensive looking clothes and the suitcase. Pushing a cab and specially out of that air terminal cab rank, you get so you know luggage. You're loading bags into your cab and loading them out of it and you get to know. They's the kinds people have when they're going economy and they's the kind when they're going first class. That was a first-class suitcase if I ever hefted one."

"Did you happen to notice the airline tag fastened to it?" the inspector asked.

The cabbie gave that careful thought. He took off his cap and scratched his head. He scowled. He concentrated.

"No," he said at length. "It didn't have no airline tag fastened on it. It come off or she'd took it off before she came out to the cab rank."

# CHAPTER 4

That was it for the night. There was all sorts of routine, of course, and much of that had already been in process. The body had gone off to the Medical Examiner. The specialists had combed the death scene. The scrapings and dustings would be worked over in the police labs. The checkout of Jack Sterling's past associates and known enemies had been begun. Before knocking off for the night Inspector Schmidt issued the orders for the rest of what he wanted done. His demands were anything but modest.

He wanted rundowns on Jacques, on Rudy, and on all the hairdressers employed in the atelier. He also wanted one on Paddy, the P.J. bartender. He further wanted the Feds queried for anything they could give him on Jack Sterling's associations and activities during the years they'd had him under their care. He most particularly wanted to know what, if anything, they could give him on Mary Smith. He wanted to know where they had been keeping Sterling.

In addition he ordered a further check on Mary Smith, an exploration of the possibility that fingerprints brought up in the apartment might serve to identify her. He ordered a check of all airlines that operate out of Kennedy, La Guardia, and Newark. He was looking for any record of a Mary Smith on a flight into New York that evening and of a Mary Smith who might have flown out again the same evening.

I listened to all this, and I had a question.

"What about the big redhead?" I asked.

"We'll talk to Vice Squad about her in the morning," he said. "Her or him."

"Man in drag?"

"We've had them. On the descriptions we've got, it could be."

"But," I said, "if somebody knew that Sterling would go with a man, wouldn't sending a guy around in drag be setting up unnecessary obstacles?"

"Sterling could have been expected to see through it, and it could have been known that he went for guys in drag so it wouldn't put him off. Also we don't have to think about it as drag. How about disguise?"

I caught it. "They're going to be seen together," I said. "When the police start asking questions, you'll be told he was a woman. It was supposed to put you off the trail."

"One way of figuring it," Schmitty said.

"You have another way?"

"A woman—big and husky and tough. There's nothing simple about S-M. It can go all sorts of ways."

"Swinburne," I said.

"Who's he?"

"He was an English poet. He used to go to a house in St. John's Wood where there were two women who flogged him."

"No kidding?"

"Well-established historical record," I said.

"You writers are more peculiar than anybody," Schmitty said.

"We're like anyone else. We're all kinds. Swinburne was an odd one."

"So was Jack Sterling. I need to know just which oddity."

It seemed to me that we had it pegged. "Mary Smith," I said, "is big and husky. The redhead is big and husky. I would guess that Swinburne's women in St. John's Wood were also formidable."

"Swinburne? What was the rest of his name?"

"Algernon."

"You're kidding."

"Algernon Charles Swinburne."

"People fasten a name like that on a kid and they expect he won't grow up peculiar?"

"Look," I said. "It had to be something pretty powerful to bring Sterling back to New York. What says it wasn't Mary Smith? If she was giving him what he wanted, he could have been crazy enough about her to follow her back to New York. He would have followed her anywhere."

"There's only one thing wrong with that."

"His going with the redhead? Mary was out of town. The redhead came along. Married men do it all the time. The wife's away or he's on a business trip. The opportunity comes his way. He can be crazy about the little woman, but she's not around and he fills in."

"And it can be said that in that way masochists are no different from traveling salesmen. No argument there," Schmitty said.

"Then what is wrong with it?"

"He's so nuts about this Mary Smith that he follows her anywhere."

"That's what I said."

"He follows her to New York where she spends the least of her time and where he knows he'll be committing suicide. Why doesn't he stay where he is? It could be she spends more of her time there. It could hardly be less. On the other hand, if she's always on the move, never many days in any one place, why does he follow her here for just the one night and then let her take off without him? It looks like he wasn't following her everywhere she goes. He followed her to New York and then stayed on here without her. More than that, even on the one night, from the looks of the body, she didn't give him what he needed before she took off. He hadn't had it recently, and he'd only begun having it when he got the knife."

I gave up on it. Inspector Schmidt had made his point. The thing was still too wide open. It was no good building an attachment to any one hypothesis. Schmitty was keeping all possible channels of his thinking open. I had encountered this with him many times before. He does it, but I can't. It's too much like juggling. If I ever tried to keep five plates in the air, it would get me nowhere but knee deep in shattered crockery.

In the morning I was out of coffee. I had been meaning to pick some up the day before but had forgotten it. I'm not going to pretend that Jack Sterling or my assignment to watch for him in P.J.'s had put it out of my mind. It happens too often. Things go out of my mind quite on their own. It may be that I am careless about these small domestic matters because it's never any big deal. One of the many amenities of the neighborhood where I live is a little mom-and-pop store around the corner on the avenue. It opens early and closes late, and it stocks all manner of great things of which great coffee isn't the least. It's too

easy to pop around there any time. Who needs to remember?

I pulled on a shirt and slacks, stepped into loafers, and
trotted out for the coffee. To reach the store I have to cross
the side street on which I live. As I told you, the address
Froman had given was the apartment house just opposite
my place. When I came out to the street there was no
traffic coming through, so I went straight across. It's another habit I can confess to. I'm a confirmed jaywalker, but
it's a neighborhood habit. We all do it.

In any event before I started toward the avenue, I
crossed the street. It was only after I was across that I saw
him. It was a man. He was coming down from the avenue,
walking toward me. He was walking with a slight limp. He
had his left arm across his chest, cradling it protectively in
his right hand. His thick lip could have won the envy of a
Ubangi. His shiner was a masterpiece of color and form.
The man was the perfect picture of the walking wounded.

I was taking only casual notice of him, feeling a small
wave of human pity, but then he looked straight at me and
he reacted. I've never gone around scaring people. I'm a
mild-looking type. I pack no visible menace, but this guy
took one look at me and he could have been wanting to
jump out of his much-damaged skin. Stopping short, he did
a quick left and took his turn at jaywalking. He hurried
across the street. It was then that, even past all the damage,
I registered on him. This was Christopher Froman. His
sudden decision to cross over was taking him to the side of
the street where he didn't live.

It was obviously evasive action, and that took some understanding. We had parted friends the night before. I
hadn't expected that he would be avoiding me. If anything,

I'd had a slight concern lest the man become a nuisance. At the bar in P.J.'s he had acted like the most eager of police buffs. That kind, when they know of my association with Inspector Schmidt, often do become nuisances. Anything about crime in the newspapers—and when is there a newspaper without something about crime?—will bring them to my doorstep with questions. They come to tap me for the instant solution and the inside dope, neither of which I'm likely to have.

I crossed back toward him. He hesitated. I could see that he was considering countering me with a return crossing to his own side of the street, but he gave up on that. Instead he tried to walk past me as though he had never known me. A moment of merciful impulse told me to leave the poor guy to his pain, but I rose above it. I accosted him.

"Froman," I said. "What happened to you?"

He gave me a what's-it-to-you look and followed it with a quick glance up and down the empty street. Only then did he put on the counterfeit of belated recognition.

"Oh, Bagby," he said. "For the moment I didn't recognize you."

It couldn't have been feebler, but I suppose he had to say something.

"If you don't mind my mentioning it," I said, "you're changed more than I am."

"You've got two eyes to see out of," he said, making a neat recovery. "I have one that's temporarily out of commission."

"You look terrible. What hit you?"

"I know I look terrible. I hate being seen like this."

"Don't give it a thought," I said. "I've seen worse. What happened?"

"On my way home from P.J.'s last night two muggers jumped me. I was stupid. I tried to fight them off. I'll never do that again."

"They get anything?" I asked.

"Every last thing I had on me."

At the bar I had noticed his wristwatch. I have an eye for conspicuous waste and when it is one of those thin-as-a-dime quartz jobs that looks much too thin for that much money even though it does do everything short of making waffles, I take notice. When the Duchess of Windsor said, "You can never be too rich or too thin," she might have been talking about one of those watches. So now I was noticing it again. Do people who go for such baubles keep spares lying around the house? When we left him the night before, it had been at an hour when all stores are closed. Now, it was early morning before any stores had opened. I know I was on my way around the corner to that mom-and-pop job for my pound of coffee, but they don't sell watches, not even Mickey Mouse watches.

"Have you been to the police?" I asked.

"What for? For tea and sympathy? What could they do for me?"

"Possibly nothing," I said. "Even probably nothing, but if you don't give them a shot at it, it's going to be certainly nothing."

"You can tell Inspector Schmidt if you like."

"I'll do that."

"Tell him I was mugged. Tell him I resisted and got beaten up."

"Is that the way you want him to have it?" I asked.

"What does that mean?"

"You didn't lose everything."

"Was it you or was it me, Mr. Bagby? Who's going to know better?"

"You didn't lose your beautiful watch," I said.

"They overlooked that."

"You were lucky."

"I don't feel lucky."

"With police protection you could feel luckier," I said.

"Where do I get police protection?"

"Inspector Schmidt."

"That's a crock and you know it," Froman said. "In this town what happened to me can happen to anyone. Sure, the police could do more than they are doing, but they can't put a bodyguard on every man, woman, and child in the city."

"They can put one on a man who might be a murder witness," I said.

"I didn't witness anything."

"That's not the inspector's opinion."

"The inspector can keep his opinion," Froman said. Obviously on the brink of telling me where Schmitty could put it, he took a hold on himself and left the words unspoken.

"I'll tell the inspector," I said.

"If you must, and while you're at it, you can also tell him that I am in no shape to look at anything. Tell him, sorry, but I'm not well."

"Also frightened?"

"If you were me and it happened to you, wouldn't you be frightened? It will be a long time before I can get over looking back over my shoulder."

"Like now," I said. "Relax. There's nobody around to see you talking to me."

"Dammit. Leave me alone."

With that he crossed back to his own side of the street, and I went on to get my coffee. Mrs. Plotnick was tending the shop. That's their pattern. She does the early opening. He does the late closing. She wanted to talk. She'd heard about the terrible thing that had happened to the poor man up the avenue.

"You know, Mr. Bagby," she said. "I think we should have known he was in trouble," she said.

"You knew him?" I asked.

"We sort of knew him. He was a customer, but peculiar, most peculiar."

"Tell me about him," I said.

"Your inspector will want to know," she said. "That's why I spoke of it to you. We don't gossip about customers. We never do even though there are things we could tell, they'd make the hair stand right up on your head, but we mind our own business. We don't talk about anyone."

"Of course, but this is different."

"It is. You know? We never saw him."

"He was a customer?"

"On the telephone. He would call and order sandwiches. It was always sandwiches—lunch, dinner, even breakfast. He'd order, and he'd ask what it came to. When the boy would take his sandwiches up to him, he never opened the door. The boy never saw him. The money would be there on the hall floor right by the door and through the closed door he'd tell the boy to leave the bag on the floor by the door and take the money."

I thanked her for telling me. I assured her that it wasn't gossiping. It was something Inspector Schmidt would need to know. I told her that she had done her duty as a good citizen.

"We never gossip about anybody," she said.

I zipped back home and, even before I put on the coffee, I phoned Inspector Schmidt.

"You've lost a witness," I said.

"I didn't have a witness except maybe the two in a small way, Rudy and that guy, Froman. So what? Why? Who?"

"Froman. He just told me to let you know that he won't be looking at any pictures."

"Yeah. He was headed that way. It was a cinch Paddy would talk to him first chance he had him alone. I hoped maybe Paddy wouldn't be so persuasive."

"He's got a thick lip and a black eye. The eye's a beaut, swollen shut. He's also nursing his arm and limping a little."

"Did he tell you where he got all that?"

"He says he was mugged on his way home from P.J.'s last night. His story is he resisted and got the hell beaten out of him."

"Bull. He isn't the type to resist. The guy's a marshmallow."

"Or perhaps a jelly bean," I said. "He told me he lost everything he had on him, but he's still wearing that watch of his. Did you notice it? It's the kind that goes for thousands. He says the muggers just happened to overlook that."

"He came across the street and volunteered all that garbage?" the inspector asked.

"He volunteered nothing," I said.

"You sweated it out of him, Baggy?"

Ignoring that crack, I went through the full play-by-play. You've already had that—the evasive action and the evasive talk.

"He wasn't going to say Paddy worked him over," I said.

"Did you ask him that?"

"No. Would it have been the right question?"

"No. It would have gotten you no answers, not since the persuasion had already been applied and he has been persuaded."

"I've been having a big morning," I said. "I have something else for you."

"Not Rudy?"

"No."

I fed him what I'd had from Mrs. Plotnick. The inspector made no comment on it until he had heard me out.

"That fits with what we've had from Jacques and Rudy," he said. "It also fits with Sterling's problems as we knew them. He had to be crazy to have come back to town. He would need to have been a lot crazier to go around letting himself be seen. What needs thinking about is how it could have been that he both was and he wasn't. He had the good sense to hole up in the apartment and not open the door to anyone, but he also had the bad judgment to put himself on exhibition every evening in that joint. How do you make the two things fit together?"

"Claustrophobia," I said. "He did the wise thing for as long as he could stand it. Keeping Rudy out; keeping the delivery boy out—that was easily done. He didn't have to fight himself to do that much. That wasn't any deprivation. Come the evening, though, the itch to be out and around would get to be too much for him. He made the mistake of figuring P.J.'s to be the kind of place where he'd be safe."

"Okay," Schmitty said. "That kind of a place and the nearest one. He could go there and, coming and going, he'd have the least time out on the street. But it's your neighborhood. You know it."

"What's this I'm supposed to know?" I asked.

"Within two blocks in almost any direction from his

hideaway you've got at least a half a dozen bars so much alike that you can't tell one from another."

"I've never been in any of the others," I said, "and for just that reason. They are all the same. There's nothing to choose between them except that P.J.'s is nearest."

"That's all right for you. You're not laying low. Nobody's after your hide. The word gets around that any evening you want to find Bagby he'll be there, hanging out in P.J.'s. You can find him there."

"That's not so. Mostly I go weeks without ever setting foot in the dump."

"That's you. It isn't Jack Sterling. Sterling set foot in it every night. What you do is beside the point. It was what he was doing. If he had to get out and sit in a bar because he was going stir crazy, why didn't he do the rounds of all those immediately available places? He would probably have gotten caught up with anyway, but he made it all too easy."

I was thinking. "What's happened with Froman," I said, "could be all to the good."

The inspector wasn't ready to take any such sanguine view. "If we catch up with the big redhead," he said, "I still might get an identification out of Rudy, but Rudy didn't get more than a passing look. Froman had time to study the dame, and he did study her."

I couldn't argue that, but my thinking had been taking another turn.

"It seems to me," I said, "that Froman has handed you Paddy or, if you like, Paddy has handed you himself."

"Because Paddy shut Froman's mouth for him?"

"Who else?"

"Too many other people else," Schmitty said. "The four

of us weren't alone—Froman, Paddy, you, and me. Let's
say that someone in the bar had put out the word that anybody who wanted Jack Sterling could find him there."

"That's become pretty obvious, hasn't it?"

"Just plain obvious. Okay. It could have been Paddy
who passed the word, but it could just as easily have been
one of the customers. It could have been Jacques or Rudy
or any of the other guys in the barber shop. They were seeing Sterling go out and head into P.J.'s every night."

"None of them would have known that Froman was
talking," I said.

"That's right. So that makes it look as though in this
connection we can forget about the barber-shop contin-
gent. It still remains that some customer in the bar could
have passed the word on Sterling. Such a customer would
have been interested in anything that was being said between us and Froman and Paddy, interested enough to give
it an ear. He wouldn't have had to have heard much to
know that Froman was sounding off."

"When you began talking to Paddy," I said, "Froman
was hanging near. He got into the act. I grant you there
were other customers in the place, but nobody up real
close. I very much doubt that there was anyone within
earshot."

"To hear you or me or to hear Paddy. We were holding
it down, but Froman wasn't. Froman was enjoying himself
too much. He was broadcasting."

Again it was something I couldn't argue. Inspector
Schmidt's words brought it back all too clearly. The man
had been having a great time. He had been carried away. It
hadn't been until he had begun backtracking that he'd been
less than stentorian.

"Yes," I said. "I see what you mean. It doesn't pin it on Paddy, at least not in any way you could call beyond question."

At that point, of course, Schmitty did it to me again. No sooner do I reach the place where I have the delusion that I'm firmly grooved into the lines of his thinking, than he shakes me loose by handing me a glimpse of at least one other avenue he's keeping open.

"Even if it was Paddy who beat up on him—and Paddy was steamed enough to do it," he said, "that doesn't necessarily tell us that Paddy had any part in fingering Sterling for the killer. Paddy doesn't have to be worried about anything more than his joint's good name."

"Things are never as simple as I like to think they are," I said.

"The most thing this one isn't is simple," Inspector Schmidt said.

"Want me to come down to headquarters?" I asked.

"No point. I'll be clear of the paper pushing by noon. What kind of a lunch does that P.J.'s do?"

"Edible if you hold still for a quiche or eggs benedict."

"Hamburgers?"

"Yes, but you'll have to lean on them if you want them to leave off the sauce bearnaise."

"Okay. I'll lean. I'll pick you up at your place a little after twelve."

"I'll be here."

I gave the morning to letters and stuff I had on my desk. Reading all the signs, I had a feeling that it could be some time before I would be getting back to the typewriter.

Inspector Schmidt turned up as promised. We didn't go straight out to lunch. Although I had nothing further to tell him, the routine had come through with a few facts. It was still too early for anything like a full autopsy report, but the ME had passed on to the inspector what could be determined from surface examination. As Schmitty had surmised, the knife thrust had come early in the game. The evidence indicated that it had not been preceded by any kind of sexual union.

The check of the airlines had produced some results. There was a record of a Mary Smith who had been a passenger on a Minneapolis-New York flight. The flight time fitted perfectly with the timing we'd had from the cab driver. There was, however, no record of a Mary Smith on any flight out of New York that same night.

"Then she did hole up in the john till the cabbie had taken off," I said. "She's still in town, and you can wait for her to come home."

"I can wait," Schmitty said, "and much good it's going to do me. I'm betting she's not going to come home."

"She has her clothes and stuff up there."

"Expendable. The stores are still selling clothes."

"But you can still pick her up," I said. "She'll be going to her bank or something."

"If she's in town."

"The airlines say she didn't fly out."

"How much does that mean? There are trains. There are buses. They don't keep any records of passengers' names. Maybe she owns a car or, picking up a car hire, she could have driven out of town. There's not even any guarantee that she didn't fly out that night. On an international flight where she'd have to show a passport, there might be a record but then only if she had a passport under the Mary Smith name. With a Mary Smith there's never any knowing. A Mary Smith can have a lot of names, a real one and any number of phonies. On a domestic flight there wouldn't even be that. She could have given any name and flown anywhere in the country."

"Yes. That's true," I said. "So what you have out of the airline check is pretty worthless."

"Not entirely. We've got Minneapolis. The town where the Feds had Sterling tucked away isn't far from Minneapolis. A flight from there to New York would have been made out of the Minneapolis airport."

"You're getting cooperation out there?" I asked. "They'll be looking for her?"

"For what it's worth," the inspector said. "Let's go eat."

The idea had been lunch at P.J.'s. So when we had walked around there, I headed for the door. The inspector pulled me away.

"We're not starving," he said. "We can take a couple of minutes."

"Sure. Anything you say. A couple of minutes for what?"

"For asking Jack something."

We went on down to the atelier. Jacques was doing something wierd and wonderful to a guy's hair. We had a short wait till he would break loose from that. Since Rudy was more available, Schmitty tried to make do with him while we waited.

"This P.J. place down the block," he said.

"Yeah."

"Do you ever go there?"

"For what they soak you for a beer? Am I crazy?"

"What about your boss? Does he go there?"

"I don't know. You got to ask him."

Completing his work of art, Jacques saw his spectacularly coiffed customer to the door. Schmitty buttonholed him and over his protests of a customer waiting, drew him into the back room.

"Just a few questions. You come up with quick answers and you'll be back at your chair before you're even missed."

"People don't like to be kept waiting."

"So let's not keep them waiting. P.J.'s down the block? Do you ever go there?"

"When you're in business, Inspector, it's a good idea to patronize your neighbors. I have some very good customers I first met in P.J.'s"

"I thought it would be like that," Schmitty said. "I could see right off that you're a good businessman. Times when she's been in town, did you ever see your tenant, Mary Smith, there?"

"Oh, frequently. She'd be there for meals."

"The last time she was in town, that one night when she'd brought the boyfriend home with her?"

"They had dinner at P.J.'s that night."

"The two of them together?"

"Yes."

"Since last night have you heard from her?"

"I never hear from her except as she comes or goes. Otherwise it'll just be the first of the month when I have her check. Today's nowhere near the first of the month."

"So she hasn't come or gone? She hasn't been through to you about the stuff she has up there in the apartment?"

"No. Why would she?"

"I've been thinking if she wasn't coming back, she might get in touch to arrange with you about getting her things packed up and sent on to her."

"Not coming back?" The way Jacques took that gave every indication that it might have been a brand new thought to him. "Yes. When she finds out what happened, I can imagine she might not want to go on living in the apartment. I could understand that. I know I wouldn't be comfortable living in a place where something like that had happened, but that wouldn't be until she'd heard about it, would it?"

Inspector Schmidt offered no direct answer to the question. It might well have been rhetorical. In any event the inspector chose to take it as such.

"If she does come back or you hear from her in any way, I'll expect you to let me know right off," the inspector said. "Even if it isn't until the first, when her check comes in, let me know. Hold the check and envelope for me. I'll want to photocopy the check and I'll want the envelope. Also, if this time you don't have a rent check, let me know."

"She never misses," Jacques said. "She's never behind."

He was, nevertheless, quick to promise full cooperation. He had that customer waiting out front.

At P.J.'s we had to wait for a table. Ordinarily the inspector would have dragged me away to the nearest quick-and-dirty where we could be served without waiting, but this was a time when he had reason for patience. Waiting for a table at P.J.'s means roosting at the bar. There was no place where Schmitty would rather have been.

Paddy was behind the bar. He was busy and showing no indication of wanting to be sufficiently less busy to take notice of our arrival. I'd been having some slight misgivings about the inspector's luncheon plan. Paddy had been working late the night before. I had been wondering whether we mightn't find that at lunchtime he would be off duty.

"He works long shifts," I said.

"Owners do. In these joints, if the owner takes off at all, it won't be at meal time."

"Is he the owner? I didn't know."

"Yes. It's his place. His name's Jensen—Ole Jensen."

"Paddy's an alias?"

"More like a trade mark."

*"Non du zinc,"* I said.

"Zinc?" Through his long association with me the inspector is up on *noms du plume.*

I filled him in on those little Paris cafes where, because, the bar tops are metal, the joints are known as zincs.

"Oh, yes," he said. "You and Froman, you've been to Paris."

The time came when Paddy could no longer put off coming to our part of the bar and asking what he could give us. We ordered. It could have been that Schmitty was getting addicted to Perrier. He ordered and he grabbed the moment.

"Seen Froman today?" he asked.

"No. He hasn't been in. He's never here for lunch. Brunch on Sunday, yes, but never for lunch on a weekday. Lunchtime he'll be downtown."

"In the shape he's in today?"

"What shape? I ain't seen him."

"After he left here last night he got beaten up on his way home."

"Mugging?"

"So he says."

"I guess he ought to know."

"Ought to know what to say." That was Inspector Schmidt's amendment.

"It happens all the time. A guy's on the street and he looks like maybe he's got a buck on him. I don't have to tell you, Inspector. You cops sure enough know about it even if you ain't doing anything to stop it."

"It also happens all the time to guys who are witnesses," Schmitty said. "It makes them have a change of mind about being witnesses."

"What was he a witness to?" Paddy asked, as though he didn't know.

"He got a good, long look at the woman I want," the inspector said.

Paddy, making a long reach for heavy humor, offered some obscene suggestions of what the inspector might want her for. Schmitty, in the interest of building good will, went along with the joke.

# CHAPTER 5

At that point a table opened up and Paddy told us to take it.

"Come and sit with us," Schmitty said. "We need to talk."

Working up a great air of regret, Paddy explained that he couldn't leave the bar. There was business to be done. He had thirsty customers. He had no time for talk. As it happened, however, he wasn't working the bar alone. There was a second barman with him. This guy spoke up.

"Go on, Paddy," he said. "I can handle it alone. They're mostly eating now."

His eager helpfulness earned him nothing from Paddy unless it was not-too-covert dirty look, but Paddy relinquished his bar apron and came and sat with us.

"What gets me," Schmitty said, "is its happening so quick. How could anyone have known that Froman was was talking?"

Paddy caught that one on the first bounce. He wasn't waiting for any spelling out.

"If you're looking at me, Inspector, then take a good look." Palms down he spread his two hands flat on the table. "Look at my hands," he said. "They look like I been beating up on anybody?"

There wasn't a mark on his hands—no puffed knuckles, no cuts or scratches. I had seen Froman's face. Having done that kind of damage, no man could come away from it without showing at least some small mark on his hands. Punch a man in the mouth with enough force to puff his lip, and you're lucky if you don't come away with a skin break where you hit a tooth. Even if you are that lucky or the skin over your knuckles is that tough, you'll be showing a mark the next day.

"It can be done," the inspector said. "All it takes is brass knucks."

That, of course, was nonsense and the inspector knew it. He'd had from me a most exact description of Froman's facial injuries. It had definitely not been a brass knuck job. There were no cuts around the eye and no cut lip. Brass knuckles cut. Froman was giving every evidence of having taken a brutal beating, but it had been no more than a bare-fisted beating.

Paddy went white. Hastily he pulled his hands back off the table. It was no good leaving them out there to make an exhibition of the way they had begun shaking.

"Geez, Inspector," he said. "What would I beat up on him for? What's it to me?"

"That's what I'm waiting for you to tell me," Inspector Schmidt said.

"It was nothing to me."

"Don't give me that, Jensen," Schmitty said. "You weren't going to know anything, but Froman spoiled that for you. You going to tell us you liked it?"

"It was nothing to me," Paddy repeated.

"We were here, Jensen. We could see how much you liked it."

"Look, Inspector," Paddy said. I still have trouble thinking of him as Ole Jensen. His Irish saloon-keeper act made Paddy seem so much the better fit. "Look. I run a nice place here and I'm doing good with it, real good. I got nice customers. I got regulars, and they're all ladies and gentlemen. I run a nice, quiet, refined place, and that's the way the people who come here like it."

"So?"

"So a lot of things, Inspector. First of all Mr. Froman. He's one of my regulars. He's got a lot of friends come here. I mean friends they come here all the time. I beat up on him and then what happens? No time at all and I'll be in here talking to myself. Maybe I wouldn't lose all my customers, but I'd lose the ones they're the backbone of the business, the ones that come here all the time."

"That's why I believe you, Jensen," Schmitty said. "I saw that about you from the first. You're a businessman. You're all business."

Looking past the words, Jensen wasn't liking what he saw.

"You can say it, but you don't act like you're believing me."

"You're wrong. I do believe you. You never laid a hand on Froman, much as you may have been itching to do it."

"Yeah. That's the rest of it. Why would I have a lot rather he hadn't opened his mouth?"

"I've been asking myself that," Schmitty said. "Want to tell me?"

"Like I been saying, I run a nice place here. So this guy starts coming in."

"Which guy is that?"

"The one from up the block here, the one got himself murdered the other night."

"Jack Sterling."

"That his name? I never knew his name."

It couldn't be that he hadn't learned the name. He

couldn't have been ignoring the morning news. He was overplaying his ignorance. The inspector seemed to be letting that pass.

"Jack Sterling," he said. "That was his name back when he used to live here in New York."

"I wouldn't know. He was just a customer who was coming in here every night, but not for any long time, just for a few hours every night."

"From the time he came back into town till the night he was killed," the inspector said.

"If you say so, Inspector. All I know is when I seen him in here and when I ain't. Okay. He looked like a fruit. Maybe he was and maybe he wasn't. You can't always tell on looks, and anyhow what's the difference? They let them in churches. You going to keep them out of bars?"

"In a nice, quiet, refined place," Schmitty said.

"He was quiet. He behaved himself. He didn't bother nobody, and it ain't like he just come in off of the street."

"He didn't? How did he come in?"

"The first time? He come with a lady. She's real nice. She's an old customer. He came in with her for dinner."

"Mary Smith?"

"That her name? I don't know her name."

"She has an apartment over the barber shop. It was in her apartment he was killed."

"Geez. Was she there?"

"No, she was out of town. I'm told she's out of town a lot of the time."

Jensen-Paddy thought about that for a moment or two. "Yeah," he said. "That would be it. She's like one of our regulars and again not a regular. She'll be in here, sometimes lunch and dinner, sometimes one or the other, but every day. Then it's maybe a couple of weeks or more we don't see her. I guess it's she's a regular whenever she's in town."

"She got back to town last night."

Jensen froze up. There was a long silence. When he broke it, he was scowling and his tone was belligerent.

"I been playing straight with you, Inspector," he said. "I don't know what the hell you're after."

"I'm after everything you can tell me about Sterling and about the woman he picked up here the night he was killed, and that's both everything you want to tell me and everything you don't want to tell me."

"There's nothing I don't want to tell you, but you keep playing tricks with me. You said the lady was out of town and now you say she was back in town. If you want to know was she in here last night, then I can tell you. She wasn't in here."

"Right. I'm sure she wasn't."

"So why do you say . . . ?"

"It was one night she was in town and she didn't come in here. It was after dinner when she arrived. It could have been she needed a drink. It's likely she did, but if so, she had it somewhere else. You won't know about that. Let's get back to what you do know."

"Like what?"

"Like the last night Sterling was here. The pickup. That redhead Froman saw—now she wasn't the kind that hangs out in a nice, quiet, refined place. Guys who run nice, quiet, refined places are careful to keep her kind out. Also, when anything like that walks into the place, the good businessman can't tell me he fails to take notice of her. He takes notice and he keeps his eye on her. He watches for the first move that will give him an excuse for asking her to leave."

"Okay. I seen her. I spotted her the minute she walked in."

"Last night you couldn't remember her."

"I didn't want to remember her. I didn't want anyone else remembering her either. That's not good for business."

"You let her stay. You let her do her stuff."

"Look. It's not like you think, Inspector. It ain't easy. A big, tough dame like her, hard as a rock, you can't just jump right in and tangle with her."

"Too big and too tough for you to handle, Jensen?"

"You run a bar, Inspector, you got to know people. Her kind, she's going to start screaming. She's not going to go just because you tell her to. You're going to have to throw her out, and she'll be scratching and biting and wrestling you all the way to the door. It's nothing you can handle nice and quiet."

He worked at it, covering the whole situation. He didn't like the woman being in his nice, quiet bar, but he had tried to deal with it the best way he could. After all, she hadn't created any kind of a disturbance. There had been nothing wrong with her but the way she looked. He had seen her come in and he had expected that she might have one drink, if even that, and go right out again.

"They come in once in a while," he said. "Pretty quick they see this ain't a place where there's going to be anything for them. They walk right out again and go looking for a joint where they see it's maybe a better chance they can make a score."

"But this one stayed and she made her score here."

"Yeah. I didn't like it none, but again what was I to do?"

He worked at explaining what had been his predicament. He had seen happening what he had expected could never happen. He'd thought he knew his clientele. He'd been certain that the woman was going to find nothing in his place and that she would quickly become aware of the fact and that with no assistance from him. To his astonishment, she found Sterling.

"I knew nothing about the guy except that he had first come in with a nice woman, an old customer. It seemed crazy that a guy who knew a woman like that would ever go for this babe, but he was going for her. There again, though, they was quiet. He just bought her a drink, and they went to the booth in back."

"Where they felt each other up."

Jensen sighed. "If Mr. Froman says so, maybe he saw it," he said. "I don't know. I wasn't back there. Nobody was seeing it without they was trying specially to look, and it wasn't like it was a long time or any big thing. They drunk up and they pulled out. I was glad to see her out of here. And that was it. It was no big thing."

"Last night," Inspector Schmidt said, "it was very big to you that I shouldn't know about it."

"Look, Inspector. Something's happened up the block. They's cops up there, police cars, all that. A police inspector comes in here to ask questions. All I'm thinking is it's up the block. It ain't in here. For business reasons I don't want no part of it. It comes out that a babe she was in here and she picked up a guy—that's publicity I don't need. It don't give the place the kind of name it's got to have. If there's going to be dirt around, I don't want it spreading into my place."

"So for business reasons you put out the quick word to get Froman clammed up?" the inspector said.

"What would I do that for? He'd already opened his big mouth. He'd already told you. I was stuck with it. I was just going to have to take the stink and hope it wouldn't hurt business too much. So what then? Was it I was mad at Froman and I wanted to get even with him? Getting mad is never good business, Inspector."

"And you're just a businessman who never forgets the bottom line?"

"You can bet your ass I am. Froman walks out of here and he gets mugged. That's my lousy luck. Even like that it's no good for me. People think there's muggers hanging out in the street outside my place, they'll look to go some place else where maybe they'll feel safer. It's my lousy luck it happened when he left here. I don't bring anything like that down on myself. I'd have to be crazy, Inspector."

He had a good argument there. I could see that it wasn't going down very well with Inspector Schmidt, but that's the way the inspector is about coincidence. Coincidence, he has told me often enough, is an easy out when you are confronted with circumstances for which you cannot easily find a rational explanation. We've discussed that many times, Schmitty and I. I'll argue that, unlikely or not, coincidences are never impossible. They do happen. You can't rule them out. So I knew just what the inspector was thinking. You can't rule them out, but no competent investigator will jump at accepting them. He must go all out to satisfy himself that there is no connection.

I was thinking back to the suggestion Schmitty had himself made to me, the possibility that there had been someone in the bar who had heard Froman's noisy chortling about the big redhead, the possibility that it had not been Paddy but someone else who had passed the quick word that Froman was talking.

I was wondering whether Schmitty was still keeping that in mind. He seemed now to be all too solidly convinced that it had been Paddy. I told myself it was only that it was

Paddy he was working on, not on that unknown, problematical someone else.

So far as the food and drink part of it went, we had long since finished lunch. There had been several times when Jensen had turned in his chair to look over toward the bar with what he hoped could be taken as a businessman's eye. He had been wanting to see such traffic in that direction as might have given him a pretext to pull out from under Schmitty's questioning.

When the table had opened up for us, however, it had been the beginning of the petering out of the lunch-hour business. Long before the inspector had finished with Paddy things had died down to the place where we were having the premises to ourselves. It was going to be pretty much like that until the cocktail hour would bring the bar to life again. There might be the occasional person dropping in through the midafternoon hours for a quick drink, but it was the time of lull.

Out in the street I asked my question. "You don't believe him?"

"If all he has on his mind is publicity and good name and all that," the inspector said, "I can believe him. He's right that he had nothing to gain and everything to lose from Froman's getting beat up. All the same, I'm going to have to be convinced that it's all he has on his mind."

"What else?"

"Sterling was set up. Jensen's nice, quiet, refined saloon was used for setting him up. Maybe it was done without Jensen's cooperation and maybe not. If it was not, then Jensen has a stake there that's big enough to make him forget all about being a good businessman."

"You're going past the thought that he fingered Froman," I said, "to speculate about the possibility that earlier on he had fingered Sterling."

"Something like that. I'm waiting for the boys to come through for me with the dope on who Jensen is and where he's been."

"There's something completely crazy about this thing," I said.

"It's been crazy from the beginning. For Jack Sterling to have come back to New York—that was crazy."

"Yes, but once he did come back, the routine he followed makes no sense."

"In his situation," the inspector said, "there was no routine he could have followed that would have made sense."

"But still . . . He's come back to town. This Mary Smith has him set up in her apartment. Okay. He was going to hole up there and nobody would know he was back. So then the two of them go to P.J.'s for dinner."

"Either he thought or she persuaded him that P.J.'s would be safe," Schmitty said. "Nobody was going to recognize him there."

"Then what about the story I had from Mrs. Plotnick? He has the one meal at P.J.'s with Mary Smith. She goes off after the one night and he never goes back for another meal. He stays shut up in the apartment and lives on sandwiches. He is trusting no one—not Rudy, not Plotnick's delivery boy. He doesn't want them to even so much as see him."

"Once you recognize that the man had to be an idiot to come back at all," Schmitty said, "then you have a whole flock of reasonable possibilities. You have to remember that we're talking about what could be reasonable for an idiot."

"Like what?"

"Like he doesn't want Mary Smith to know what he is or that he has a problem back here. He's taking a chance when he goes out to dinner with her, but he has no way of getting out of that. He takes the chance that once, but later, with her gone, he doesn't have to go on taking it."

"Then why did he go on taking it? Not safe to go out for a meal, but safe after dinner? Okay. He's an idiot, but that's too idiotic."

"It was too idiotic. That may be the reason why he's dead. He took the chance that once. He's determined he won't take it again. Day after day he gets himself through the morning and afternoon holed up in the apartment, but then he's had his supper sandwiches and there's the whole evening stretching before him. He gets stir crazy, and night after night he breaks down and he takes the chance again and again. Come morning each new day, a little sanity breaks out. He promises himself he won't do that crazy thing again, but by evening he's again ready to forget his good resolutions. It's like a guy who's trying to stay on the wagon or maybe to stop smoking."

I had to concede that for an idiot that could have been reasonable behavior.

"Yes, I suppose," I said. "Then there was also sex rearing its ugly head. Mary Smith wasn't here to service him. That would have been a factor."

"A big factor," the inspector said. "It's always a big factor. So that's one way it could have been. In the same way, though, it could be that Mary Smith knows all about him. She doesn't like sandwiches, and she persuades him that P.J.'s will be safe as churches. The people that go there—nobody could possibly recognize him. He's convinced. So he keeps on going to P.J.'s."

"But not for meals."

"He tried it the once. He didn't like the food. Also it could have been money. The joint isn't cheap."

"The Plotnicks aren't cheap either."

"Even expensive sandwiches eaten at home are a lot cheaper than sitting down to a meal in a restaurant. It doesn't even have to be a restaurant like P.J.'s."

That much was also unarguable.

"Good enough, but since the idiot's relaxed enough to set himself up at P.J.'s every evening, why is he so uptight about Rudy and the delivery boy?"

The inspector laughed. "Baggy," he said, "you're just no good at thinking the way an idiot thinks. P.J.'s is such an elegant, refined, upper-class dump. Only the best people go to P.J.'s. The best people aren't Jack Sterling's problem. Should he be thinking that he has anything to fear from the best people? Rudy and the delivery boy are lower class. He's not taking any chances with them."

"And he thought his big redhead was best people?"

"She picked him up at P.J.'s, and isn't that where the best people go? Jack Sterling wouldn't know the difference."

"Not when he was greatly in need," I said.

"That's the big factor."

"But he was wrong about P.J.'s."

"Equally possible that he was wrong about Mary Smith."

"Not on what I saw of the way she played it," I said, "and not on what you've had from the cab driver. She came rolling up in that cab. She saw the cop in the vestibule. She saw police cars. She had a quick realization that she had gotten herself mixed up with a wrongo, and she got away from there quick. She'd made a mistake in Sterling. She wasn't hanging around to get mixed up in anything."

Schmitty shook his head. "No," he said. "She knew enough to have an instant recognition of what was going down. A cop in the vestibule, police cars—they didn't have to be there for Sterling. There's the third-floor-front. There's apartments on the fourth and the fifth. There's the barber shop and there's Jacques on the second floor. I'm interested in her recognition of what was up. It can be that she knew it was going to happen. It can be that she's the one who set Sterling up."

"If so, why would she have come back at all?"

"That's one of the questions that needs answering," the inspector said.

We had gone back around the corner to my place, and all the time we'd been talking the inspector was at the window, looking out at the apartment house across the street. As was his custom, as soon as we had come in, he had rung headquarters to let them know where he was. So, when the phone rang, it was for him. He was on the phone for a considerable time and he was saying nothing. He was just listening, and it was obvious that little of what he was hearing was to his liking. It began with a look of unhappiness, but the look quickly turned grim, full of tamped-down anger. When he did speak, just from the way he asked his question, I knew that he was asking only out of the most forlorn hope that in some way he could escape believing what he had been told.

"You're sure of this?" he asked. "You've checked it out?"

There seemed to be no escape.

"Yes," he said. "I know. It's just that there was a time when he was a good cop."

He hung up and, coming away from the phone, he

moved heavily. It was as though some weight that had been put on his spirit had added to his physical weight.

"Trouble?" I asked.

"It may be a break in the Sterling killing," he said.

If a break in the case had been the last thing he could ever have wanted, he couldn't have mumbled the words more unhappily.

I didn't have to ask anything more. I knew what it had to be that was eating him. Checking into the people on whom five years back Sterling had blown the whistle, one of the inspector's boys had come up with someone whose career in the department had gone down the drain in the spate of Sterling's talk. The guy would be off the force. In Schmitty's book he would long since have been written off as a wrong one. There are, however, degrees of wrong, and murder is the ultimate degree. For Inspector Schmidt receiving such intelligence would have been a fresh blow, a wound reopened. He took only a moment or two before he shook it off.

"Our friend, Ole Jensen," he said, "is a cousin."

I could make nothing of that. All the assumptions I'd been making were now knocked out of the park. If the news he'd had was handing him Jensen, I couldn't see how that would make him unhappy. There was also what he'd said on the phone about someone who had been a good cop. It was not possible that then he could have been talking about Jensen. If Jensen had been this one-time good cop, Schmitty would have known him on sight. So there was that word "cousin." I was taking it for a bit of police slang I'd never heard before.

"What's a cousin?" I asked.

"Your old lady has a sister. Her sister has a son. He's your cousin. Since when do I teach you English?"

"I was thinking slang," I said. "Who's the cousin?"

"You wouldn't know him. His name's Williams—Cal Williams. He was doing right well in the department until Sterling spilled how well Williams was doing on the side. The guy was in the racket. He was in with both feet or, if you like, with both his greedy hands."

"And he's Paddy's cousin?"

"Paddy's mother's sister's boy. It's fully documented. No possible mistake."

I sighed. It was mostly out of sympathy for Inspector Schmidt. Of all the ways that this could have gone, he now had it in the way he could have wanted least. To a lesser degree, of course, I was sharing his feeling. I had never known Cal Williams, but through the years I have been close to the inspector I have come to know cops. All through the force there are men who are my good friends. I like cops and I respect them. When a cop goes wrong, you can feel anger and contempt, but that doesn't stop you from also feeling pain.

"So this wraps it up," I said.

Schmitty was quick to reject that. "It's a lead," he said. "It's only a lead."

I had to concede that strictly speaking it was no more than that. It would have to be followed up. All the connections would have to be made. The connections would have to carry through to the big redhead. Schmitty could say it was no more than a lead, but the fact remained that it was the only lead he had. I didn't have to tell him that. He knew it at least as well as I did, and like it or not, he would follow it and he would do it relentlessly. If anything, he would make himself push harder than he might have done in following a happier trail.

"Back to P.J.'s?" I asked.

"Jensen will keep. First we go across the street."

"Froman?"

"He's sick," Schmitty said. "You call on the sick. It's the nice thing to do."

"Customary among the best people," I said.

The inspector was himself again. He was either that or he was indulging himself in a postponement of his embarkation on the Cal Williams trail. Across the street we inevitably tangled with the apartment-house doorman. Schmitty asked for Froman's apartment number.

That wasn't the way they did it in this security-conscious establishment.

"Who's calling?" the doorman asked.

"Never mind who's calling. We'll go up unannounced."

"I'm sorry, sir. Nobody goes up unannounced."

"Inspector Schmidt. Police. Mr. Froman will be expecting us."

"One moment."

The doorman walked away from us, but only as far as the switchboard mounted on the wall behind the lobby reception desk. Schmitty followed after him close on his heels. The doorman didn't like that, but he was not prepared to do anything about it. I thought the inspector was bent on listening in on the doorman's end of any exchange he might be having with Froman. I was wrong. The inspector stayed with him only long enough to see him plug into the switchboard.

Without waiting for the doorman to start speaking, Schmitty moved briskly across the lobby to the elevator. It was standing at the lobby level with its door open. We entered it and the inspector pushed the button for the fourteenth floor.

"Fourteen-E," he said.

I chuckled. I've always known that Inspector Schmidt is a resourceful man, but he can still astonish me with a revelation of some new dimension of his resourcefulness. All he had wanted at the switchboard had been the number on the socket into which the doorman plugged his line.

The elevator door remained open. The elevator didn't move. The inspector hit the button again and still nothing happened. He tried another button. This time it was the one marked:

DOOR
CLOSE

He did no better with that one. The doorman came away from the switchboard. He hesitated for a couple of moments, just looking at us. Then he moved out to his front door and shouted at us from there.

"Come out of that," he said. "You won't go up."

"Who says we won't go up?"

"You won't go up because Mr. Froman isn't home."

"He'll be home to us. What's wrong with this elevator?"

"It's controlled from the concierge's desk. It won't go up unless he sends it up and he's not sending it up."

There was a man sitting behind that lobby desk. He was just sitting there. He was doing nothing. He was leaving it to the doorman to carry the ball.

"You've got tenants who'll be wanting to use it," the inspector said.

"That's why you're coming out of there."

"But we're not."

"You have to."

"What do you plan to do about it? You want to call the cops?"

"If I have to. Yes, that's just what I'll do. I'll call the cops. They'll get you out of there."

"Before you make the call, you'd be smart to come back here and take a look at my identification," the inspector said.

"Bring it out here."

"We're not going anywhere. We like it where we are."

"You're right about that much, mister. You're not going anywhere."

The man behind the desk came to life. He said something to the doorman. We couldn't hear what was said, but the man was gesturing toward a battery of lights he had on his desk. It was a good guess that he was telling the doorman that he was having calls for the elevator from upstairs.

Scowling, the doorman capitulated. He came across the lobby. He was swallowing his rage. He tried to be persuasive.

"You're not getting anywhere," he said. "You're just making trouble."

Schmitty had his ID out. He pushed it at the man.

"You called up to Mr. Froman," he said. "He told you he was not at home to Inspector Schmidt. Now you go back and tell Mr. Froman that I'm on my way up because I don't want to have to put him under arrest, and I'd rather not waste the time going off to get the warrant for his arrest because all that time there will be a killer loose with Mr. Froman well up in the victim line. Once he understands that he is going to be at home to me one way or the other, he's going to want to have it this way. You better also tell him that I know what's worrying him and that it is my professional opinion that he's just making it more dangerous for himself by keeping me hung up down here where people can see me."

The doorman said nothing. He expressed himself only by sweating. He walked away from us and went to the desk. He spoke a few words to the so-called concierge and the elevator door closed. As the door was closing, we could see the doorman. He was back at the switchboard. As soon as the door had clicked shut, the car started up.

"He's calling Froman to tell him he couldn't keep you out."

"I hope he's giving him my message. Otherwise Froman can complicate my life by taking off by the service stairs or the service elevator."

"He's at least that scared of talking," I said.

The inspector probably didn't hear me. He was grinning at the elevator's battery of non-functioning buttons.

"No thirteenth floor," he said. "Froman should expect to be unlucky. Unless you're smart enough to know that calling it fourteen doesn't change it from being thirteen, it's just lousy arithmetic."

# CHAPTER 6

The elevator disgorged us on the floor marked 14. All the apartment doors up there were shut. The inspector made straight for 14-E. There he leaned on the bell. Through the door we could hear the ringing. The door remained shut. The inspector gave it his fist. That produced no better result. He tried banging with the butt of his service revolver. That did have an effect. The door of 14-D opened.

A woman stood in the doorway. She was so fashionably thin, you could slice cheese with her profile.

"Poor Mr. Froman," she said. "He's not answering."

"He's in?"

"Oh, yes. I know he's in. It's frightening his not answering, isn't it?"

"Why frightening?"

"You may not know it, but he was hurt last night, badly hurt, and now, if he's not answering, he must be in there unconscious. You know, he must be in a coma or something. We'll have to get Murphy up with his master key. There was Mr. Henderson. He was a very old man down on the seventh floor. He was very old and, when he didn't come out of his apartment for days, Murphy went in and he found the poor old man dead. It was a coronary, and he'd died in there all alone and nobody knowing for days until Murphy went in. Of course, Mr. Froman isn't old like that, but with his injuries . . . Yes, that's what I'll do. I'll call down and have Murphy come up."

She had one of those high-pitched voices that can't be beat for carrying power. It carried through Froman's walls or through his door. He opened up.

"Murphy won't be necessary, Mrs. Carter," he said. "It is just that I am not seeing these people. So if they will simply go away and stop disturbing everybody . . ."

He tried to push the door back shut, but that involved moving more than the door. He would have needed to move Inspector Schmidt as well and that was beyond his strength. Instead Schmitty pushed his way in and I followed after him. As I was shutting the door behind us, I could hear Mrs. Carter's protests.

"But you mustn't do that," she was saying. "Mr. Froman told you he doesn't want to see you. You can't just go pushing your way in. You shouldn't have been allowed up."

We moved away from the door and from the sound of the lady's voice. Reluctantly, Froman trailed after us.

"I'm sick," he said. "I'm in no shape to see anyone or to talk to anyone. You had no right to come pushing in here. I haven't done anything."

"You know better than that, Mr. Froman."

"What have I done? Tell me that. What have I done?"

"Last night over in P.J.'s you said things your friend Paddy didn't want said. Before you were through, you began to realize that you'd been talking out of turn, but it was too late then. So you were taught a lesson."

"I don't know what you're talking about. I doubt that you do either."

"It was a painful lesson and with it came the threat that,

if that wasn't enough to silence you, there would be more. Just what were you promised, Mr. Froman?"

"You're talking nonsense."

"Was it that you would be killed or was it just that your tongue would be cut out? You're up against people who have done it both ways. We've seen them where a man has been murdered and his tongue cut out as well. That way it's a message to anyone else who might be thinking of talking. There's no knowing which came first, the cutting or the murder. Not knowing gives people pause."

"I was just mugged." Froman tried, but he couldn't achieve anything like a convincing sound.

"That's what you told Bagby. You're talking to me now."

"I'm not talking."

"Because you fear for your life. You handled this badly, Froman. The way you played it, our coming up here got to be a big, conspicuous public performance. You can't hope that it won't be known that we've been up here. You've made it certain that it will be known. Do you expect your muggers to believe you when you try to tell them that, closeted here with me, you didn't tell me anything?"

"That's why you should have left me alone. What you've done is criminal. You've put me in the most terrible jeopardy."

"You've been in jeopardy, Froman, ever since you opened your mouth last night," the inspector told him. "You saw too much and you talked about it. From that time there has been safety for you nowhere, no safety apart from what I can provide for you."

"You knew that," Froman said. "So show me the safety you provided for me."

"Hindsight, Froman, hindsight. If I had known what I know now, I would have given you such care as you haven't had since you've been out of diapers. I didn't know, but now I do. You need police protection and I want to give it to you. I want to move you out of here where they know where to find you. I want to hide you away. I want to give you bodyguards. I want to keep you safe, Mr. Froman."

"I'll never be safe again," Froman said. "You've fixed that."

It was more a moan of self-pity than an accusation.

The inspector told him he was wrong. He worked at convincing the man that his danger was no more than temporary.

"You help me catch up with that woman you saw with Sterling, and that will be it. You'll be all right. There will be nothing to be gained then from messing with you. As long as you have something to tell that you haven't told, there is a profit in silencing you. Once you've told everything you know, there is no longer any advantage in shutting you up. It's as simple as that."

I could have said it was in no way that simple. Jack Sterling had done his worst and nobody had ever pretended that telling all had put him out of danger. There had been revenge and there had been making an example of the man who had talked. Inspector Schmidt had told me that much himself. I was, of course, saying nothing. I was on the inspector's side. I could feel pity for Froman, but not so much that I would want to spike Inspector Schmidt's guns.

"But I told you everything I saw," Froman said. "I told you last night. I don't know anything more."

"You can identify the woman. You may be able to pick

her out of the pictures I'll show you. When I catch up with her, you'll be able to identify her."

"Why are you leaning on me? Paddy saw her. He got at least as good a look at her as I did. Why don't you work on him?"

"You remember her. He says he doesn't."

"Hogwash. I was there. I saw him. His eyes were practically dropping out of his head, he was looking at her so hard."

"Sure he was, but you're a willing witness and he isn't."

"Who says I'm willing? I'm not willing."

"You should be, Mr. Froman."

"Why me? Why me and not him?"

"Because he has an ax to grind and you haven't," the inspector said. "Paddy is involved. His minimum involvement is his not wanting it known that undesirable people frequent his bar. Now, on no more than that it isn't likely that he would have had you beaten up. So there is a strong possibility that he is even more deeply involved. It was no time at all before the word was put out on you. Hasn't it occurred to you that it had to be Paddy who set up the attack on you? Or did he do his own knuckle work?"

"It wasn't Paddy. I was mugged on the street."

"You know better than that, Froman, and so do we. Think. Who could it have been if it wasn't Paddy?"

"You," Froman said.

I haven't often seen Inspector Schmidt rocked back on his heels, but with that pronoun Froman did it. Schmitty took a moment or two to think about that one.

"I want you to talk to me. So I set some guys to beat you up and warn you not to talk to me?"

Froman explained. We said we were police, but he had

no way of knowing that we were. So far as he could know, we weren't. So far as he could know, we'd been in P.J.'s the previous evening trying to find out if anyone had seen the woman and had taken enough notice of her to remember her, trying to find out if there was anyone who needed to be silenced. We had found Froman.

At the beginning of that I saw Schmitty start for his pocket to bring out his ID. He quickly thought better of it. Froman was so enamored of this line of thought he was throwing at us that the inspector chose to hear the man out as Froman pursued it to its conclusion. The man didn't realize that he was giving himself away, and Schmitty had no intention of stopping the flow until he'd had the whole of it. It was only when Froman had fallen silent that Schmitty showed him his credentials. Froman moaned.

"So it leaves Paddy," Schmitty said, "or someone else who was in there last night. Think back. You weren't holding it down. You were plenty audible."

Froman tried to backtrack. "I don't know why we're talking about all this that didn't happen," he said. "I was mugged. That's all."

"I'd like to leave it at that, Mr. Froman," the inspector said. "It would be easy to leave it that way because then there would be no reason for you not to look at my pictures. You have one eye you can see out of now. The other eye isn't going to stay swollen shut forever. It will be opening pretty soon. It would be nice if I could leave it with just having you describe the guys who mugged you, getting you to look at the pictures, and getting you to pick that big redhead out of the line-up."

"I won't."

The inspector ignored the interruption. "That might

have been possible if we could have just dropped in on you quietly without drawing a lot of attention to ourselves," he said. "I could have taken the chance on your being okay until I'd had everything I need from you. My problem is that I just cannot afford to play it that way. I can't take the chance on losing you, and you've fixed it so that there's too good a chance that I will lose you."

"You shouldn't have come up here. You should have left me alone. I asked you to."

Froman was whimpering.

"Unfortunately, Mr. Froman," Inspector Schmidt said, "I couldn't do that. I couldn't for two reasons. There is a murderer walking around loose, and it's my job to find that murderer. So that's one reason. The other is that, when I can, I should be preventing murder. That's also part of my job. So I had to force myself on you if it was only to protect you from the results of your own bad judgment. Your safety depends on my putting you under police protection."

Froman didn't like it, but the inspector at last had him convinced. He listened to Schmitty's account of what he proposed to do about him. Before we would leave him, the inspector was going to install a precinct cop in Froman's apartment. That would be temporary.

"That's just for while I'm getting the necessary arrangements made," the inspector said. "As soon as I am ready to move you, you will be taken from here in an ambulance. You will be taken to a hospital, but you won't stay there. You will leave the hospital in another ambulance for the place where we'll keep you hidden until I have this thing cleared up. You can see that we will be taking every precaution against the possibility of your being followed."

He was trying to be reassuring, but he was only partially

successful. Froman remained with some misgivings and, watching the man, I could see those misgivings grow to a revised terror.

"I've read today's papers," Froman said.

It was not just a simple statement. The man was offering it as an argument. I was slow to pick up on what he could have been driving at. I had also read the papers. The Jack Sterling murder had been given a big play. The stories told of his being found murdered. They included the lurid details of the condition of the body. Beyond that they dug into the past to rehash the five-year-old scandal. The papers had printed everything they had and everything they could learn. There was no mention in any of the stories of P.J.'s or of Froman. While I was puzzling over what Froman might be thinking, Inspector Schmidt was quick to read the man's mind.

"The police officer who will be with you until you can be moved," he said, "and all police officers who will be anywhere near you or who will even have any knowledge of you will be handpicked by me. They will be men who have never had any connection with anyone who was fingered by Sterling. They will be men I know well, and they will be completely reliable."

Froman showed no evidence of Schmitty's assurances having erased his doubts. He shrugged it off. Obviously it was his thinking that, like it or not or even trust it or not, he was stuck with it. He had nowhere else to turn. The FBI? From his reading of the papers he would have known that some of their men had been criminally involved and had been brought down by Sterling's testimony. So what could have been left to him? Army? Navy? Marines? Air Corps?

The inspector used Froman's phone to call precinct and

specify the man he wanted detailed to him. I knew the lad he'd chosen. He was a young cop, no more than two years on the force, but he was a good one.

It was only a few minutes before he arrived. He came in chuckling.

"Inspector, sir," he said, "Mrs. Carter, the lady lives next door, she thinks I'm here to arrest you. She's going to be disappointed when I don't pull you out of here with the cuffs on you."

"We do our best," Schmitty said, "but we can't hope to keep all the taxpayers happy."

He gave the kid his instructions and we hauled out of there. Across the street in my place, Schmitty hit my phone to set up all the arrangements for Froman's removal and safe keeping. That took time and, while he was on the phone, he allowed himself a bit of relaxation. He shucked out of his shoes. A relaxed Inspector Schmidt must always be a shoeless Inspector Schmidt. Way back in his rookie days he had pounded a beat. His feet have never allowed him to forget it. As soon as he had finished on the phone, however, he climbed back into his shoes. That was a sign I could read.

"Where do we go now?" I asked. I knew we were about to be on the move.

"Yorkville," Schmitty said.

"What's in Yorkville?"

"Second Avenue. Somewhere a couple of blocks above Eighty-sixth Cal Williams has a little business. Back when he was on the force, it was his hobby. Now I hear he's making a good living out of it. He repairs and restores old furniture. His probation officer couldn't be happier about him."

I groaned. "They never learn, do they?" I said.

"That," Schmitty said, "remains to be seen."

In detection you must keep an open mind. The inspector has told me that often enough, but he has never failed to amaze me with his capacity for keeping his open. I've never known him to do a conclusion jump. He's always pulling me back from the ones I do.

It was a small shop, and from the street it was unprepossessing. It looked cluttered and shabby. Inside it smelled of wood and wax and glue, but I quickly recognized that it wasn't a showroom. It was a workplace. There was just one man in the shop. Though he couldn't have failed to hear the bell that jangled with the opening of his shop door, he didn't raise his head to see who had come in. He was bent over what he was doing, and he was not allowing himself to be distracted from it. He was occupied with the blistered veneer on a drawer front. His task was a delicate one. I watched in fascination the way he was going about it.

His hands were big and you could have thought they would be clumsy, but they moved with magnificent precision and control. His was the light touch of a concert pianist's pianissimo. There was no limpness in it. Muscular strength lay behind its lightness. I know enough about eighteenth-century cabinetmaking to recognize a piece of museum quality when I see it. It was not only the veneer he had under his hands. It was the other pieces he had in the shop as well. It was obvious that Cal Williams had the custom of high-priced decorators and major collectors. His probation officer had every reason for thinking he was doing well.

"I won't be long," he said, speaking without ever raising his head to give us even a quick glance. "I have to stay with this now or I'll ruin it."

"We can wait," the inspector said.

We waited and we watched him work. Seeing a man exercise a great skill in any craft is never boring. Schmitty seemed to be as absorbed in watching as I was. It was only a few minutes and then with a nod of satisfaction Williams came away from it. He turned to speak to us. His movements were easy; but, at sight of the inspector, he tightened.

"Inspector Schmidt," he said. "I've been expecting you. I hoped not, but I have been expecting you."

"But you waited for me to come to you," the inspector said. "You weren't volunteering anything."

"I had nothing to volunteer, and I hoped."

"Hoped what?"

"Jack Sterling murdered, Inspector. Could I think I wouldn't be one of the suspects? I could hope, but I had to know better."

"That's all?" the inspector asked.

"Did I need more?"

"You didn't need it, but it's likely you had it."

"What do you want to know, Inspector? Did I kill Sterling? No, I didn't. Did I have anything to do with getting him killed? No, I didn't. I went out of line and I took the fall for it. So now that's wiped clean. Not all wiped clean, I suppose. I am on probation, but I'm doing okay. I was a dope, but that doesn't mean I'll go on forever being a dope. A man can smarten up, Inspector. I paid for what I did and I'm still paying, though this part of it isn't rough on me. Sterling has also been paying."

"Paying?" Schmitty said. "He turned State's evidence and got off. You did time."

Williams shrugged. "I did mine inside," he said. "Sterling served his outside, but being where he was hidden away—for him that had to be the same as serving time. Just the fact that he was crazy enough to pull away from it and come back to New York tells you that much."

"You have a cousin," the inspector said.

Williams winced.

"I have a lot of cousins," he said. "We're a baby-having family."

"Cousin Ole."

"Two of them named Ole," Williams said. "The way we keep them apart, one's just Ole and the other one's The Better Ole."

He wasn't old enough to be remembering the World War I cartoons. It would be a family joke handed down from an earlier generation.

"Cousin Ole who calls himself Paddy for professional reasons."

"He couldn't call his place O.J.'s. He wouldn't want O. J. Simpson suing him."

"Okay," the inspector said. "So now we're talking about the same cousin. When did you speak to him last?"

"Yes, Inspector. He called me. When was it—a week ago, about then? He called to tell me he had seen Jack Sterling. Sterling was in Ole's place eating dinner. Ole even told me what Sterling was eating."

"He called you that same night, while Sterling was still there?"

"He said he was still in there, still eating. He hadn't gotten to dessert yet, but Ole knew what he had ordered for dessert."

"Let's not horse around," Schmitty said.

"I know. You're waiting for me to tell you what I said and what I did."

"That's right, Williams. I'm waiting."

"I told him that for me Jack Sterling was history and a piece of history I wanted to forget. I didn't want to see Jack Sterling and I didn't want to hear about Jack Sterling. I told Ole that I wished he hadn't called me. I wished he hadn't told me. Sterling's being in town was something I didn't want to know because it was a cinch that something would be happening to Sterling and it would be something bad and I had to be far away from it."

"And that's all?"

"That's all except that I also told him that for his own sake as well as mine he should stay far away from it, too. Forget he saw Sterling, forget he knew who Sterling was, keep his mouth shut and not say anything about Sterling to anyone. I also told him that he would be smart to give Sterling his strawberry cheesecake quick and get him out of that place of his. I told him it would be even better if he had him out of there before the cheesecake. I told him there are guys would be catching up with Sterling, and it wouldn't do him and his business any good if they caught up with old Jack in his place. All right. I was thinking that it wouldn't do me any good, but sure enough it was true for Ole too."

"You haven't seen or talked to your cousin since?"

"No."

"He hasn't called you? Not even after Sterling was killed?"

"The one time he called, I told him he shouldn't have done it. I told him that the last thing I wanted would be that anybody should be keeping track of Sterling for me. I told him how it is on parole. You have anything at all to do with any of the wrong elements and you break it. I told him I didn't want to hear from him anymore. I didn't want him putting me back inside."

"Guys who would be catching up with Sterling," the inspector said. "Who?"

"You know the list as well as I do, Inspector. All the guys who took the fall that time. Me, I'm keeping away from them. I'm not seeing them. I'm not hearing from them. I don't know who's where or what any of them are doing, and I don't want to know. I'm clean and I'm staying clean. I've got a good business. I'm making a good buck. I'm happy with what I'm doing. I like doing it. It was what I was going to do come retirement time." He managed a wry smile. "Retirement time came early for me," he said.

"How well did you know Sterling?" the inspector asked.

"Not well. Not ever well. I knew he was in on the shakedown racket just like he knew I was in on it. We never worked together. Some of the guys who were in on it used to go together. They'd go drinking or to the horses or like that. I didn't. Maybe you won't believe me, Inspector. I didn't like what I was doing. I didn't like myself, and I didn't like any of the other guys that were in it. It was like I couldn't get away from myself, but I could stay away from them. I did."

"You never went whoring with him?"

"When I need a woman, I don't go running in a pack."

"There are men who do."

"I've never been one of them."

"Know anybody who did?"

"Yes."

"Anybody who ran with Sterling?"

"Not that I ever heard tell about."

"You didn't know anything about his sex life?"

"Really know?" Williams said. "Nothing. I had some ideas, but they were only ideas. I didn't know and I didn't want to know."

"What ideas?"

"Just to look at him, I thought he could be a queer, but just on looks you can never be sure. Both tough and queer, that's a dynamite combination. So, as much as I thought about it at all, it was just another reason for keeping between him and me all the space I could."

"You know how he died."

"I read the papers. The papers went to town on the way he died."

"Surprise you?"

"Yes and no."

"What does 'yes and no' mean?"

"It didn't surprise me that he was kinky. I'd had a hunch that he would be. But that's the kind of thing you can never know about."

"Somebody knew."

"It had to be somebody who was a lot closer to him than I ever was or at least somebody who listened to stories I never heard."

"It wasn't just the one night in your cousin's place," the inspector said. "He was back there every night until the night a big hooker came in and he picked up with her and took her home with him. That was the night he got the knife in his back."

"You sure of that, Inspector? Ole doesn't run that kind of a place."

"He doesn't and that has me asking why he should have made this one exception."

"I wouldn't know about that, but I can make a guess."

"Go ahead. Make it."

"Sterling came in that first night. Ole recognized him and he called me. I told him Sterling was a cinch to be trouble and he didn't want it in his pub. I told him to get

Sterling out of there as quick as he could and to see that he didn't come back."

"He didn't take your advice."

"Since he didn't, I can think of only one reason why. Lack of guts. What I said to him must have scared him, except that it scared him the wrong way. He was afraid to get tough with Sterling, afraid to move him out, afraid to keep him out. He was scared of the guy. The usual kind of people he gets in his joint, he'd never taken any of that kind of shit from them. A hooker comes into his place, he'll move her out double quick, but with Sterling going for her, Ole must have been scared to do anything. He wasn't going to take his chances messing with Sterling, no matter what."

That explanation didn't satisfy Inspector Schmidt. I could see how there hadn't been a chance that it would satisfy him. After all, I knew about Froman and about the beating Froman had taken.

"That's a nice place your cousin has," the inspector said. "Is it all of it his or does the mob have a piece of it?"

"It's all his. He had a bank loan to get it started. Maybe that's all paid off now and maybe not. I wouldn't know. He worked and slaved to get his own place and he swung it with a bank loan and other money he borrowed, but that other money was all from the family."

"You're family," the inspector said.

"Yes, and back when he was getting started I was pulling in money I couldn't let show. Lending it to my cousin, it didn't show, but then when I took my fall, he scraped up every penny and paid me off. I needed money for lawyers and he needed to be shut of me. You don't keep an alcohol license if it gets found out that even a little piece of your financial backing is coming from a criminal."

"That was you," the inspector said. "Anybody else who

had money to hide and was hiding it in a loan to cousin Ole?"

"It was all family money," Williams said, "and the family is clean—all of them except me. I'm the black sheep."

"Back then he was into you for money. You and he were close."

"No. We weren't particularly close. We weren't even close enough so he told me he needed money. His old lady —she's my mother's sister—told my old lady that her boy needed more money than he could get from the bank and my mother, just talking, mentioned it to me. You know, she—the rest of the family—never thought I'd have anything I could let him have. On a cop's pay how could I? I went to him and asked him how much he needed. He was surprised, but he didn't ask me any questions and I didn't tell him anything."

"But that brought you close. Lending him the money would, wouldn't it?"

"Yes. I suppose it did. When he got opened up, I'd go in there once in a while for a drink or two if I was in the neighborhood. I ate there only once. I'm a meat and potatoes eater."

"I know what you mean," the inspector said. "Did you ever bring any other guys with you or recommend the place to anybody? You'd want to help him build a clientele."

"You mean any of the others in the racket?"

"You're reading my mind."

"No, I didn't. I told you before. I was in it, but I didn't run with any of them, and even if I had, they wouldn't have been the kind of clientele he needed or wanted."

"Then you're telling me that your cousin Ole is squeaky clean?"

"He was stupid to let himself be scared of Sterling, but he's clean."

"No chance of a mob contact?"

"Look, Inspector," Williams said, "you're in a position to know. Time was when I was also in a position to know, but it's been five years now. Back when I knew, I would have said that there wasn't much chance a guy could run a bar in this town without some protection. Maybe it would be straight cash payments for protection and maybe it would be buying his booze from the right people or something else like that. Maybe the big bust five years back made the whole town clean and maybe not. I have no way of knowing. This much I do know: It's been five years now and, if it hasn't built up again, then water's running uphill. Ole runs a bar."

Inspector Schmidt set about filling him in on his cousin Ole's bad memory and on Froman's total recall.

"It used to be, Inspector, that people didn't want to get mixed up in anything dirty," Williams said. "We used to have to give them a lot of help with their remembering. Has that changed?"

"It hasn't changed, but this guy, Froman, started home from that place your cousin runs. Home is just around the corner; but he didn't get there before he was picked up, worked over good, and told that he never saw anything, he can't remember anything, and he can't identify anybody— or else. Now that was quick action, and there was nobody but cousin Ole to know that Froman had anything to tell."

That hit home. I could see that it hit hard, but Williams made a quick recovery. He hadn't been a cop for nothing. He also had a mind that was open to various possibilities. Watching him and listening to what he was saying, I was remembering that, according to the inspector, Cal Williams in his time had been a good man.

"Now, hold it, Inspector, hold it," he said. "This guy wasn't in any private place when he did his talking. He was bellied up to the bar. Just up the avenue there's been a murder. The police are all over the place. The people that set it up, they're watching. They know where Sterling had been the night he died. They know where he was picked up for it. Maybe your big redhead did it herself. Maybe she was just a decoy and some guy took over. Either way they see police headed straight for Ole's place. They wanted to know what you were learning there."

"No big redhead followed me into the bar and hung around listening," Schmitty said.

"It didn't have to be her. Also it could have been her if it was a red wig and a guy in drag. Out of drag he can hang around and not be recognized."

"That's why I haven't arrested your cousin Ole," Schmitty said, "but I have to be thinking about him."

"Yeah, and I've got to be wishing it had been some other pub."

"That, too," the inspector said. "Why was it his pub?"

"The address in the paper, where it happened, it's only a few doors away."

"Yes, the place nearest to where he was living."

"Wouldn't that be why?"

"Maybe."

"The papers," Williams said. "There was nothing about Ole or his place or this guy, Froman."

"I don't tell the papers anything they can't get for themselves unless it's something I think they need to know."

"And me?" Williams asked. "Furniture I bring to the

shop and work on it here, but there's jobs I can't bring to the shop. A wood-paneled room where the paneling needs cleaning or a repair, I have to work on that where it is. So I go into people's homes. The papers say even maybe I'm mixed up in a killing, then where am I?"

"Back inside," the inspector said. "Violation of parole."

"Just for my name getting in the papers?"

"If it comes to that, it will only be because you have been in violation of parole. I am out to catch a killer and anybody who had a hand in laying it on. I'm not out to crucify anybody. If you're clean, Williams, you haven't a thing to worry about."

"I have plenty to worry about. It isn't enough that I'm clean. I have to look clean."

"That's right," Schmitty said. "You have plenty to worry about. If you're clean, you can help me with keeping you looking clean."

# CHAPTER 7

Two P.J. meals in a row were more than could be asked of Inspector Schmidt even in the line of duty. When we pulled out of the carpenter shop, we were in Yorkville and it was dinner time. Yorkville is a part of Manhattan that has restaurants the way Iowa has cornfields. For eating you can find anything you could ever want up there—French, Italian, German, Hungarian, Czech, Chinese, Greek, Mexican, and even Brazilian. It used to be a German neighborhood, and even though everything else has infiltrated it, the German base is still there.

So when we passed a nice-looking little place where the menu posted outside listed *tafelspitz,* some ancestral stirrings of desire came awake in the inspector.

"We're here," he said. "We might as well eat."

Most times when he says that, we're outside some dingy lunch counter where the sandwich bread has long since begun to curl and the coffee is straight out of the cauldron in the opening scene of Macbeth. Boiled beef was a most welcome alternative.

"This guy, Williams," I asked over dinner, "do you think he's leveling with you?"

"I think he is," Schmitty answered, "but I'm not forgetting that I want to think he is."

"I liked him," I said. "I like his shop and I like the way

he works. A man has to love what he's doing to work that way."

"Sure enough," Schmitty said. "But back when he was a cop he acted as though he liked police work."

"And since he took the chance that wrecked that for him, you can't be certain that he wouldn't be taking the chance again?"

"A man slips once, you can never be sure it isn't something he has built into him—unreliable footing."

"Then it's only that you want to believe him?"

"No," Schmitty said. "Williams has a lot to back him up. His parole officer is sold on him one hundred percent. There are parole officers and parole officers, but I know the man Williams has got watching over him. He's a good man. He knows his job and he does it. It wouldn't be easy to snow him, and he can't be bought."

"Would he have any way of knowing whether Williams might be vengeful or not?"

"Nobody could know that but Williams himself," Schmitty said. "That's the point, though. The parole officer would know whether Williams has been reviving any of the old mob connections or if he has been setting up any new ones. It's his job to be watching for that, and he would know."

He explained the significance of vengefulness for me. Williams had slipped once but that time it had been for gain, for big money. Any involvement he might have had in the Sterling murder couldn't possibly have been for gain. It could only have been for revenge.

"I find it hard to believe that for Cal Williams, where he sits now, revenge could be a sufficient motive. There's too much to lose and nothing to gain. I could understand it if he had come face-to-face with Sterling. It would be possible then that he would burst into a rage and lose his head. He'd kill the rat with his own hands. This affair is nothing like that. It was cool. It was planned, calculated, set up, arranged. That's not revenge. That's a business proposition."

"There was no money in it," I said.

"You have to understand big business. Rackets are big business. In any big business there are some activities that are not revenue producing. The Sterling murder—unless it came out of some fresh deal he got tangled in, and I don't think it's that—the Sterling murder would be classified as overhead unless it would be personnel policy, public relations, corporate image. That's what it was for, repairing the damaged corporate image. You can't talk to the cops and stay alive. That was a proposition that had to be demonstrated."

It was Inspector Schmidt's argument, therefore, that on the evidence of his parole officer and on what we had ourselves seen of him and his shop, it was hardly possible that Williams could have had a business interest in having Jack Sterling lined up for mob execution.

"Then do you buy the notion that it wasn't Paddy who blew the whistle on Froman? It was somebody who was in P.J.'s that night watching and listening?"

"I've had that in mind as a possibility, but more and more it gets to looking like a long reach."

"Then cousin Ole moved on his own even though cousin Cal told him to keep away from it?"

"It would be that he was acting in his own interest and not for cousin Cal," the inspector said.

"He'd go that far just to protect the good name of his joint?"

"Williams put his finger on it," the inspector said. "He didn't want to bring it up, but he knows that I'd be thinking it whether he said it or not. Ole Jensen runs a bar. The possibility that anyone who runs a bar has mob protection is always good. In the case of Ole Jensen, it's even better."

"How so?"

"The mob would have that little extra leverage on him. His cousin is Cal Williams. That could be leaked in the right quarters and Ole Jensen might have one hell of a time hanging on to his liquor license."

"So he passes the word that Froman can be trouble for the mob, and he gets Brownie points for it."

"He could have been piling up the Brownie points," Schmitty said. "He tips cousin Cal that Sterling is back in town. Cousin Cal wants no part of it, Ole passes the word on his own. That earns him some gratitude, but it also has him trapped. When the big redhead comes into the place and picks up Sterling, Ole Jensen's hands are tied. He has to pretend not to notice. When Froman starts sounding off about it, it will then be a lot more than piling up the Brownie points. By then he'll be trying to cover his own tail."

"Then you're going to lean on him. It's just that you'll do it without eating his food."

"Pretty soon," the inspector said.

"You'll finish dinner first. I know that."

"And get a little more to go with if I can," Schmitty said.

In search of that little more he went to Christopher Froman. He didn't have far to go. The place where his men had Froman stowed away was a quiet, small hotel on Madison Avenue in the Eighties. If you didn't know that part of the city well, you would probably have never even heard of it, but it's a good place, even elegant in a pleasantly subdued fashion. It has, in fact, a better than average dining room and efficient room service. Froman was being kept in comfort.

The man, nonetheless, wasn't happy. They had him looking at pictures, volume on volume of them. Every hooker that had ever been pulled in, booked, printed, and mugged was there and they had him doing a study of all the likenesses.

"How're you doing?" the inspector asked.

"Getting a headache," Froman answered. "That woman isn't here."

The cop who had the care of him broke in on it.

"He hasn't looked at even half of them yet," he said.

"Keep at it," Schmitty said. "You may come on her yet."

"If I don't go blind first."

"Take a little time out. Rest and relax while you and I talk."

The inspector made it sound as though he were doing Froman a kindness. Froman wasn't ready to accept it as such.

"What do we talk about?"

"Everything that happened from the time we left you in P.J.'s and the time you got worked over."

"Nothing happened. I ordered another drink and then Paddy set one up on the house."

"Does he do that?" the inspector asked. "Seems to me it's a little old-fashioned for his kind of place."

"He never bought me one before," Froman said, "but then that night was different."

"I know it was different, but I'd have thought not in any way that would have had him setting up drinks on the house. Just how was it different?"

Prior to that evening they had never said more than a

few perfunctory words to each other. Never before had they been together that way, talking for any length of time across the bar.

"The two of you had a long talk after we left?"

"An hour and more. I bought a drink. Then when he bought me one, I couldn't very well not buy again. I'd had a drink with him. I had to ask him to have one with me."

"Naturally," the inspector said. "Then he was with you all the time after we left?"

"Wouldn't you say it was the other way around?" Froman said. "I was with him. He was behind the bar, doing his job."

"All the time? He didn't cut out even to go to the john or to check the kitchen or anything? He owns the place. He isn't just the bartender."

"No. Right after you left he went to the booth in back and made a phone call, but it was just a quick call and he came right back to the bar."

"You didn't go back there with him to listen by any chance?"

"Why would I do that? I don't read other people's mail and I don't eavesdrop on their phone calls. What do you take me for?"

"You went back to watch the big redhead."

"That was different. She was something to see. The two of them were. A man making a phone call? What could be there to interest me?"

"Nothing, I suppose. What did you two talk about all that time at the bar?"

"You know what we talked about. Paddy explained to me why he hadn't wanted to tell you anything about those two and what they did. He said you people get a hold on something like that and you'll give him a hard time. He

said it had happened only the one time, and it had been
nothing he could control but that now he would be in for
it. There was going to be police harassment, and he had
been trying to avoid that."

"And what did you say to him?"

"I told him how sorry I was that I had opened my big
mouth, but that I had gone too far with it before I'd real-
ized the spot I was putting him in. I reminded him of how I
had tried to cover up for him, telling you how it was that
I'd noticed and he didn't."

"And that got him over being sore at you," Schmitty
said. "It warmed him up to you so much that he bought
you a drink."

"No. He hadn't been sore at me. He understood. There'd
been no way I could have known what was coming down. I
didn't know what a man is up against when he runs a bar."

Opened up recurrently by the occasional probing question, Froman recalled a lot more of the talk that had
passed between him and Ole Jensen. He had explained to
Jensen that it was his duty as a citizen to tell the police everything that he had seen. He had assured Jensen, however,
that this everything didn't have to include the information
that Jensen had seen just as much as he had himself seen
and had taken at least as much notice of it.

"After all," he said, "to me it seemed that part of it was
totally irrelevant to what you had to know, Inspector."

He caught himself up and fell silent. He was hit with the
realization that he even then had been telling Inspector
Schmidt what he had decided was without relevance to the
inspector's murder investigation.

"Did Paddy understand your position? I mean your obli-
gation as a good citizen."

"He understood. He was a little rueful about it. He said

he could wish I hadn't seen anything. He couldn't wish that I hadn't spoken out."

"You made a long night of it? You were there till closing time?"

"No. I had as much drink as I wanted to hold. I pulled away from the bar to go home."

"I thought maybe Paddy left with you. You know, closing time."

"I wish he had. I might have gotten home safely if he had. He just walked to the door with me."

"He ever do that before?"

"No, but this was different. He walked me to the door with his arm around my shoulders. He was showing me that there were no hard feelings."

"Did he kiss you?"

"Now what does that mean, Inspector?"

"Never mind," Schmitty said. "You've got a lot more pictures to look at."

I could well imagine that Froman wasn't a reader of the Bible, but it seemed less likely that he'd never been to the movies to see *The Godfather*. I held back on any comment until we were out of the hotel.

"Pay dirt," I said then.

"Some nice, shiny nuggets," Inspector Schmidt said. "Phone call the minute we were out of the way."

"Plus carrying the Paddy image to the unprecedented extreme of a drink on the house," I added.

"Holding Froman at the bar as instructed over the phone and, to make sure nobody would make the mistake of working over the wrong man, walking Froman to the door with his arm over the poor sap's shoulder as agreed on the phone."

"So he called Williams a second time," I said.

"Or someone else. Let's not forget the Brownie points."

"Who else?"

"He'll tell us," the inspector said, but then he was quick to undermine it. "He'll tell us unless he's too much of a rat or he's too scared."

"He could be both," I said.

"It won't surprise me. In this business you meet a lot of frightened rats," the inspector said. "It will get to be a matter of who scares him more, me or them."

So back down at P.J.'s Inspector Schmidt set himself to be his most frightening. Paddy was at his usual post behind the bar. The inspector stopped for no preamble.

"Get one of your waiters to take over on the bar. We're going to the back where we can talk without being interrupted."

It was an order.

"I'm shorthanded. There's people here. They got to get service."

"I have more than enough on you to take you in," the inspector said. "Then the people will get even less service."

Paddy signaled one of his waiters and told him to take over behind the bar. He stripped off his bar apron and started toward the back. I hadn't expected any such instant docility, and for the moment I thought it might augur well. We followed close on his heels. There was an empty booth at the back. I was guessing it would be the one that had been occupied by Sterling and the big redhead. The inspector stopped there.

"Right here will do," he said.

Paddy ignored him and continued on back. The inspector was having none of that. He took a hold on the man's arm.

"Where do you think you're going?" he asked.

"To the telephone. To call my lawyer."

"Before you even know what I've got on you?"

"You ain't got nothing on me. That's why I'm calling my lawyer."

The inspector made no comment on that. He snapped out an order instead.

"Sit down."

Paddy sat. "What do you want from me?" he asked.

"Answers, and this time straight answers. The way they say in court, the truth, the whole truth, and nothing but the truth."

"You've had it, everything I know."

"You don't know that you have a cousin who used to be a cop? Cal Williams, your mother's sister's boy."

"What's he got to do with anything?"

He tried it on but, even while he was saying it, he was showing every sign of knowing it was no good. He couldn't make Inspector Schmidt believe that he hadn't been reading the papers with their extensive rehashes of the old scandal. They had even listed the names of all the people who had been involved. His cousin Cal's name had appeared in the list.

Inspector Schmidt said nothing. He just sat there looking at Jensen. His look was telling the man that he would have to do better. It was also telling him that he himself knew he would have to do better. That look broke the man down.

"All right, Inspector," he said. "All right. This guy, Sterling, was the informer. Cal was one of them he informed on. I know that much from the papers, but Cal's out on parole. He's got a good business and he's doing real good. He don't need no trouble and he ain't looking for none. He's learned his lesson."

"The question is, have you learned his lesson," the inspector said.

"What did I have to learn? I never been in no trouble."

"That first night Sterling came in here, you called Cal to tell him the man was back in town and eating his dinner here in your place."

"How could I do that, Inspector? I didn't know who the guy was."

"Your cousin had been on trial and this was the guy who had testified against him. You never saw him then? You didn't remember him, the guy who got your cousin kicked off the force, the guy who got him sent up? Come on, Jensen!"

He tried to go on with it and he tried to make it stick. He explained that it had been the time when he had only just opened his place. He had put everything he owned and everything he could borrow into it.

"I'd worked my ass off getting it started," he said. "I was sorry for Cal, but what the hell, he brought it on himself, didn't he? I had to stay away from him. I had to stay away from the whole mess. It could have wrecked everything I'd worked for."

That was easily punctured and the inspector stuck the pin into it. He reminded him of the extensive newspaper and TV coverage the case had been given. Day after day there had been Sterling's picture on first pages. He couldn't pretend that he hadn't been reading the papers. He couldn't have been that uninterested in what was happening to his cousin Cal.

Jensen made a last feeble attempt. "Newspaper pictures," he said. "Who can recognize anybody from newspaper pictures?"

"It happens all the time," the inspector said. "I've been looking at those old newspaper pictures. They were good and clear. Also I remember all the TV shots of Jack Sterling. Don't tell me you forgot them."

"You're a cop. You have reason to look and remember."

"And you're a cousin, but we're wasting time. I've talked to Cal. He told me you called him."

"That's a bluff. I know how you guys work."

"If you know so much," the inspector said, "tell me how I know Sterling had strawberry cheesecake for dessert."

That did it. Jensen didn't speak at once. He first had the sweat to wipe from his face and neck. He had to wait till he could work up some saliva flow against the sudden dryness in his mouth. He had to come out of shock and pull himself together.

"I had to let him know," he said.

"Why?"

It was a variation on his old theme. The inspector was right. The minute Sterling walked into his place, Jensen had known who he was and the knowledge had frightened him. The man was back in the city and of all the places he might have gone to eat he had chosen Jensen's place.

"I had to think he was out to do Cal dirty or something like that. Why my place if it wasn't because I'm Cal's cousin? Okay. I wasn't just thinking I had to warn Cal. I was thinking of myself too."

"And Cal told you he wasn't interested. Cal told you to get him out of your place quick. He also told you to let the guy know that you didn't want him coming back. Why didn't you take Cal's advice?"

"It was easy for him to say and it's easy for you to say it, but doing it would have been something else again. The

guy came in with a good customer. He was behaving himself. What reason could I have said for giving him the
heave? Should I have said, 'You sent my cousin to jail, I
don't like you. I don't want you coming in here?' "

"And the night when he wasn't behaving himself?"

"You asked me that before. They was quiet. They wasn't
bothering anybody. I thought they'd get together and pull
out. She was the kind you can't put out and have her go
quietly. She would have made a stink. I had to handle it
the way was going to be best for the business."

Even a Harvard MBA couldn't have been more business-
minded than Ole Jensen.

"Last night I came in here to ask you questions," the inspector said.

"I lied to you then. Yeah, but what else could I do?"

"A lot more, and you did it. You held Froman at the
bar. Drink on the house and a long conversation, but first
you made the quick phone call. Who to? Cal?"

"Not Cal. I don't remember who."

"Don't give me that."

"I make lots of calls. I don't remember all the calls I
make, and I don't remember which was when."

"You haven't forgotten this one and you haven't forgotten how you were told to set it up. You haven't forgotten
holding Froman till your friend had time to get over here
and to be waiting outside. You haven't forgotten that you
walked Froman to the door with your arm around him because it was set up for you to do that. Nobody was taking
any chances on working over the wrong man."

"I had to do it. I had to do it for Cal, and I had to do it
it for myself. If it come out that this guy, he was murdered,
he got picked up for it here in my place, then it was going

to sure as shooting come out how Cal Williams is my cousin, and you'd be thinking like you are thinking that it was Cal got him killed."

"And trying to shut Froman up was going to keep me from thinking anything?"

"It was a mistake," Jensen said. "I wasn't smart. I made a mistake."

"That," Schmitty said, "is the truth and nothing but the truth. I'm still waiting for the whole truth."

If Jensen had been sweating before, there's no name for what he was doing now. He gave up on mopping at it. There was no keeping up with the outpouring. Schmitty waited and watched, and before long it came, a flood of words that was not much less than a match to the flow of sweat.

He was no criminal. He was a victim. He had the mob on his back. For five years he'd had them on his back. He had been paying protection and, just as Schmitty had surmised, there had been the extra leverage on him. He wasn't like anyone else in the P.J. business. He was Cal's cousin, and he couldn't take his chances on the word being passed to the Alcohol Control Board.

"You cops pretend you knocked the whole mob out five years back," he said. "You pretend like there ain't no rackets anymore. I've got news for you, Inspector. There are rackets like there always was, and the mob that had Cal in with them is operating now like they always done. They been collecting protection from me for five years. So I called them and told them they had to protect me now. It was them killed this Sterling. Any fool would know that. So I called them and told them they was in trouble on the killing. I told them about Froman, and I told them that for that they was going to have to protect me. I'd been paying them and they go and mix my place up in their killing. What kind of protection was that?"

"You don't always get what you pay for, Jensen," the inspector said. "And it will do you no good to complain to the Better Business Bureau about them. You're old enough to know that much. They had a great reason for picking Sterling out of your place. Nothing could have suited them better. You are Cal's cousin. Cal has been having nothing to do with them since he came out. They set Sterling up here and they have us looking at Cal Williams, and that's no direction in which I could be catching any sight of them."

"They collect and collect and collect, and then they turn around and do me this way."

"So you don't owe them," the inspector said.

"I don't owe them."

"And I'm still waiting for the whole truth. You made the call. You made it to the mob, but that's not good enough. I want a name. Who?"

"I can't."

"If you don't, you're playing their game."

"If I do, I'm dead."

"Their game will have all the evidence pointing to you and Cal Williams."

"Nobody can prove anything. We didn't do anything, and nobody can prove we did."

"For Cal nobody has to prove anything. Violation of parole is enough. For you there's assault and intimidation. Proof of that much is easy, and there's no jury that couldn't be sold on conspiracy to murder."

Jensen moaned. "You don't have to tell me. Either way I'm cooked."

"So there are a couple of things you should be thinking

about," the inspector said. "If you're cooked anyway, you should be thinking about how well done you want to be. Rare? Browned to a crisp? The other is Cal. It's what you'll be doing to him."

"That's his lookout. If it wasn't for him, I wouldn't be in this fix. It's his fault."

The inspector could have questioned the justice of that. He didn't. Any appeal to Ole Jensen's better nature would have been a waste of time and breath.

"Your best bet is to play along with me," he said instead. "That way you'll have police protection."

All that this offer of police protection drew from Jensen was a sneer.

"A hell of a lot of good that did Sterling," he said.

"Only because he chose to walk away from it. He was all right for five years, and he could have been for the rest of his life."

It was a good argument as far as it went, but it didn't go far enough for Jensen. He was concerned for his life, but that concern also included his bar-restaurant. He had worked for it and saved for it. A secret move out of town to someplace where he would begin a new life under a new identity he was rating as no more than another kind of death.

"I'll take my chances on what you can prove," he said. "I'll take my chances with a jury."

There it stood, and with that Inspector Schmidt could have gone for the easy out. He could have put Ole Jensen and Cal Williams under arrest and have waited for Froman to hand him the big redhead. With that he could have called it case closed and leave it to the DA's office to take it from there. It would have satisfied the Police Commissioner and the DA. They like quick answers, but the answers need to be more than just quick if they are to satisfy the inspector.

He would have been left with too much reasonable doubt. Lawyers will tell you that reasonable doubt is of no concern to a police detective. It comes into play only at the level of jury deliberation. Inspector Schmidt calls that hairsplitting. When he puts a murder case in the hands of the DA, he wants it to be an airtight package. Other police officers rail at the courts. They see the justice system as a process in which they make arrests and the courts turn criminals loose. The inspector also is unhappy with acquittals, but he sees them as the result of poor police work whether it is that an innocent man has been charged or an insufficient case built against a guilty one.

He didn't arrest Jensen and he didn't go back to Cal Williams. It seemed to me that on leaving Jensen that evening he should have been showing some indications of disappointment and frustration. He had made his best pitch with the man, and he was coming away with little more than nothing.

"So now you're down to what Froman might give you," I said.

"Froman isn't going to give me anything."

For a man who was anticipating defeat, his tone was inconsistently sanguine. He sounded almost cheerful.

"You think he's just going through the motions? He's going to pretend he's not spotting anyone?"

"I think that he won't find the big redhead among the hookers. He might be able to pick somebody out of a line-up for me. It'll surprise me if he's good for anything more than that."

"Then you're not left with anything much," I said.

"Nothing much but a pattern," Schmitty said. "Once you have a pattern, you start fitting people into it."

He went to his desk downtown. I tagged along with him. For about a quarter of an hour it was just watching him shuffle papers. Most of what he looked at he set aside. To only a few items he gave close attention. Setting those aside as well, he shoved his chair back from his desk.

"We can call it a night," he said. "I'll be picking you up early tomorrow. How about seven-thirty? We'll be making a trip upriver."

"The slammer?"

"Tomorrow's visiting day."

I couldn't make much sense of that. The relatives and friends of prisoners in a correctional facility are compelled to wait for visiting days. Inspector Schmidt is subject to no such restrictions. He can gain entree any time. I let that pass.

"Who's up there?"

"Jim Marshall. You remember Jim Marshall?"

"I've been having memory refreshers the last couple of days. Of all the people Sterling named five years ago, Marshall was the king pin."

"Right, and in or out he's still the king pin."

"You're not thinking you can get him to talk, are you?"

"Oh, come on, Baggy! I wasn't born yesterday."

"Then what?"

"It's visiting day."

"And we're visiting Jim Marshall. Are we going to bake him a cake?"

"We're going to see who's visiting him tomorrow. We're going to get a list of who he's had as visitors the last few weeks."

"Messengers?"

"Messengers," Schmitty said, "are better than nothing. I can work on messengers. Out of messengers you get messages."

# CHAPTER 8

Up at the prison the next morning Inspector Schmidt showed no immediate interest in seeing Jim Marshall. He was interested only in Marshall's visitors. He asked for the visitors' records for the past two months. Visiting days came once a week, and he was looking for visitors Marshall had been having on days that predated the time when Sterling had first been seen after his return to New York and visitors he would be having this day, the first visiting day to roll around since the night of Sterling's murder.

He let me in on his thinking. "An operation like the job done on Sterling took organization. It wouldn't have been done except on Marshall's orders. He didn't issue his instructions or give his orders by phone or letter. Marshall's too smart an operator for that."

"Of course," I said. "It would have been a messenger or messengers."

"It had to be and that's not just a hunch. There's the pattern, the timing."

"That's what you said last night. You have a pattern."

"Sterling came back to town. His first night in the apartment we can assume was his first night in the city, and if it wasn't, it makes no difference. It would only strengthen the pattern. His first night in the apartment he has dinner in Jensen's place. He wasn't hit that night."

"He couldn't be," I said. "Not the way they set it up.

They couldn't have worked that as long as he was with Mary Smith."

"I'll buy that. We can count out the first night, but then it wasn't the next night or the next. Why did it wait as long as it did?"

"It took organizing, lining up the hit woman."

"It took organizing, but these people have ready organization for this kind of thing. When they hit, they hit fast. When night after night they have their sitting duck, they don't hang back. They don't wait."

"But they did wait."

"And that's where we see the pattern. They waited for visiting day when they could get their orders from Marshall."

I counted the days on my fingers and it worked out. It had been four days since Sterling left P.J.'s with the big redhead and took her up to the third-floor-rear. That had been the third day after the previous weekly visiting day and that visiting day had been the first after Sterling's return to New York. Now the warden's office was pulling out for the inspector the records of Marshall's visitors.

"The big redhead came up and got her orders?" I asked.

"No. Someone came up to report that Sterling had made himself available. That someone left here with the orders and organized the killer, but it was done on Marshall's orders. Marshall's a brain, and the killing was cleverly handled. The job done on Froman, on the other hand, was the exact opposite. That one was clumsy and stupid."

He didn't have to go on with it. He had me caught up on his thinking.

"This somebody that Paddy called to tip him on Froman couldn't have been Marshall " I said.

"Jensen's link would never have been direct to Marshall," Schmitty said. "It would have been an underling."

"I suppose. What I was thinking was that he couldn't have made that kind of call to this place."

"Obviously not, and there again we have the timing. That hit was made, and it was made fast on what you could say would be their normal schedule. A call to Marshall up here, even if one could have been made, and a call from him to a lieutenant back in town, even if that one could have been made, and then getting the enforcer over to be outside Jensen's in time, all that could never have been done inside an hour or a little more. Froman was taken care of on an emergency basis without Marshall's advice or consent."

"So it will be who visited him last week," I said. "You asked for a couple of months of records."

"Something brought Sterling back to New York. He didn't come on his own just to convenience Marshall. His return must have been engineered as well. To work that, somebody thought up something very smart and it's a good bet, if it is anything smart, it comes from Marshall."

"Because the people he has operating for him back in the city are anything but bright," I said. "They demonstrated that much in the way they handled the Froman threat."

"That hit was never Marshall's style," Schmitty said. "If he had ordered it, he would have had the mugging made that much more violent. Froman would never have gotten home that night. He would have been dead and his beautiful watch would not have been overlooked."

The man who had been pulling the file came along with the records. The inspector began with the one for the previous week.

"Good," he said. "Very good."

"Who?"

"Dick Warren."

"Should the name mean anything to me?"

"No, but it means the world to me."

"Mob?"

"Never proven, but that's only one of a million things we know in the department but haven't been able to prove. It can go on and on that way till one day it breaks down."

"For Warren, then, this is the day?"

"Looks like it," the inspector said. "Looks very much like it."

He was gloating.

"He's stupid?" I asked.

"A lug—stupid, faithful, obedient, and a great operator under supervision. On his own, he's more muscle than mind. Froman will know him."

"You think he was the one who worked Froman over?"

"Both on what I know about Dick Warren and on the timing."

"Then he'll be Paddy's contact?" I said.

"Again on the timing, I'll say yes. Also you have to remember that they're running shorthanded. A lot of them are still put away. Cal Williams served only the minimum before he won parole, but that's Cal Williams. He was a model prisoner, and most of these babies wouldn't even know how to be that. Also, Williams had a way of earning an honest living on the outside. That weighs heavy with a parole board."

The inspector was going through the records for the earlier visiting days. After looking at them, he was passing them one by one to me. Dick Warren's name turned up on the sheet for every one of the visiting days. That bothered me some.

"He never missed," I said.

"That's Warren. Always faithful."

"But doesn't that lessen the significance of his having been up here that one time last week? The way this looks, his visits were just routine."

"They are. They're routine like a sergeant reporting to his CO every morning for the orders of the day."

"How do you prove that last week was different?" I asked.

"No need to prove it. If a man is running an operation from up here, he has to have a steady flow of progress reports, doesn't he?"

That was clear enough. I dropped it.

"Any other name here that means anything?" I asked.

"Jane Clark," the inspector said. "I'm wondering about Jane Clark."

"Anything on her?"

"Just what's here on these records."

I took another look at all the records he had handed me. By this time I had all the sheets that had been taken out of the files for him.

"She was up here every week for the first month," I said, "and she hasn't been since. Faithful but only for a time."

"Look at the address she gave."

I looked at it. It was 500 West 74th Street, Manhattan.

"I'm looking. What's with West Seventy-fourth Street?"

"The last block down to Riverside it's the three hundred numbers. Five hundred would be well out in the Hudson River. You've got a guy in the slammer and he's visited by a mermaid, you have to take notice."

"You'd think it would have been spotted when she signed in," I said. "You'd think one time or another."

"Maybe I would think so," the inspector said. "You wouldn't because you didn't spot it even when I called it to your attention. They have a lot of people to check in on visiting days. There was a time way back during the war they had MPs guarding the Hudson River piers. Nobody got on the pier without showing a pass with his picture on it. One of the papers sent a reporter over when a lot of people were being checked in. He showed a pass with King Kong's picture on it. He was passed on through."

"Some young draftee with little or no training," I said.

"Maybe. So what will it be up here. First of all, up here the emphasis has to be more on checking parcels than on checking people. They don't want a visitor bringing in a gun or a knife. Also the guy doing the checking is likely to be a local. He isn't a city boy. He won't know New York well enough to know how the numbers run on the West Side."

"I can understand that," I said. "What I can't understand is this woman risking an impossible number. She's giving a fake address, but she could give any kind of a valid address that isn't her own. Why would she take this kind of chance?"

"Jane Clark," Schmitty said. "It doesn't have nearly as much of a smell as Mary Smith, but since I can't believe in mermaids, it does have me thinking about Mary Smith. Mary Smith is out of town more than she is in. Her New York pad is East Side in your neighborhood. Can't it be that she doesn't know much about what there is over there west of the park? She took a number out of the air and hit on five hundred. It's the kind of number that out of the air jumps into your mind. It's also easy to remember for the next time."

That was something to think about, and I did my thinking aloud.

"She flew into New York from Minneapolis. It was out around there that Sterling was hid away. She found him and she worked it out some way to get him back to New York. She took him to P.J.'s, got him established there, and then she left town. If it was that way and it was she who set him up, why would she come back?"

"She didn't stay," Schmitty said.

"But she did come back. That makes no sense."

"It doesn't. When I catch up with her, that'll be one of the things I'll have to ask her—why she didn't make sense."

He returned the records to the warden's clerk. Visiting time wasn't to begin for another couple of hours. Finished with the records of visitors, Inspector Schmidt now wanted to talk to Marshall. There was no problem about that. He was summoned and it was only a few minutes before he was delivered. I was pretty sure that I had seen him in that time five years back, the time of the big bust. I had certainly seen newspaper pictures of him then. He had, however, been only one of many while Jack Sterling had been unique. Sterling had been the star of the act and, as I've already told you, Sterling had an extraordinarily arresting and memorable face.

Now that I was confronted with Marshall, I found that he stirred no memories. He was too much of the type. He looked tough even though it was smooth tough and sleek tough. He was well barbered and well manicured. He carried himself with easy confidence and even with some

dignity. He had about him the air of command. He could
have been a general or an admiral, a captain of industry or
a captain of finance. That he was, in fact, a captain of
crime I knew, but it made no difference. He had that captain look.

Inspector Schmidt told him to sit down.

"You're wondering why I'm here," he began.

"No. I see the papers. I've been expecting cops."

"Me?"

"You're a cop."

"Homicide."

"A rat got knocked off. I'm not arguing. That's called
homicide."

"He wasn't just any rat. He was the rat that put you
here."

"Could I forget it?"

"You couldn't and you couldn't let him get away with
it."

"If you're waiting for me to say I'm sorry he got his, I
can't. I'm an honest man. I don't lie."

"Not about anything?"

Marshall smiled. If he wasn't thinking that he was in
command, he was putting on a great act.

"Little white lies," he said. "We all do, don't we?"

"Okay. Who did it?"

"The papers don't say. Like the man said, all I know is
what I read in the papers."

"You give orders and you don't know you're giving
them?"

"I'm here, and being here makes me a paper tiger. I'm
the bird with clipped wings. I got framed. I got sent up. Justice is blind. When it came to me, she was deaf, too. So I'm

here and I'm paying for what I never did. I had the bad luck to go up against a jury that didn't know from anything. They didn't know that you can never believe a fag."

"You knew he was?"

"I know what I read in the papers. The papers say the way he died. You want to tell me a man that's a real man dies like that? He goes looking for rough trade, and he gets himself some that's rougher than he bargained for. If I was a cop, I'd be down in the city smelling around the leather bars."

"That was obvious from the first. That was where you wanted us to look."

"Mister, I don't give a shit where you look. I hope you never catch the fruit who knifed him. That bird's done me a service. You find him, I'll pin a medal on him."

"Dick Warren," the inspector said.

"Mister, you're crazy. Dick hates fags. Fags disgust him."

"Warren is up here every visiting day."

"He's a friend, a good friend. Just because a jury gets a guy wrong, that doesn't lose him his friends."

"If he's big enough, it doesn't lose him his clout either."

"In jail a man is clean out of clout. Even if I had an organization, and I never did—I was a legit businessman—but even if I had an organization, now I'm here, and here a man has nothing."

"You must like it here," the inspector said.

"You think I'm crazy?"

"Not crazy enough to get you off on any insanity plea but crazy enough to stick yourself with one hell of a long sentence tacked on to the time you're doing now. It's going to be Murder One this time."

"With me up here and him down in the city?"

"It's a great alibi, but alibis don't work for the man who makes the plan and gives the orders."

"You can find another dumb jury, mister, but you won't find one dumb enough to believe anybody orders sex crimes. Sex crimes are done for kicks, and who goes for second-hand long-distance kicks?"

It went on and on without going anywhere. Eventually the inspector gave up on it. He had them take Marshall away.

"That didn't come to much," I said.

"I never expected it would."

"Then why did you bother?"

"You have to try. You don't give up without trying, and there was all this time I had to kill."

He looked at his watch.

"Almost an hour before visiting time," I said.

"No good running it any closer. We'll thank the warden and get out of here," the inspector said.

I expected that "here" would be the room they had given us for the confrontation with Marshall, but it wasn't. We went all the way. We didn't stop till we were outside the prison wall.

"You were going to see who came to visit Marshall today." I thought I was reminding the inspector.

"We'll stay out here and see."

"Visitors for other prisoners," I said. "How are you going to know which might be his?"

"I know Dick Warren when I see him."

"He could have more than one visitor."

"He could. You'll be watching with me. If you see anyone you recognize, tell me right off."

"Who could I recognize that you wouldn't?"

"Lots of people. Somebody maybe who hangs out in Jensen's place, that dame who gave the cabbie a hard time."

"Mary Smith?"

"If she wears her mermaid's tail hanging out," Schmitty said, "I'll spot her for myself. She's likely to keep it tucked up under her skirt, and then I'll have to rely on you."

That was it. We hung on outside the gate and watched the visitors arrive. They began gathering there well before the time, and I didn't enjoy watching them. They were a sad-looking lot. There were old women, worn and shabby. They carried shopping bags and market baskets. It seemed to me that I could smell the pies they'd baked for their inmate sons, but that might have been my imagination. There were old men and there were young people too, but there wasn't a one of them who wasn't carrying the look of pain and misery. I was seeing them as the victims of crime. They were, of course, not the direct victims. Crime had touched them through ties of love or ties of blood. It was hard watching them because there wasn't a one among them who could draw from me anything that wasn't pity.

The opening time for visiting hours finally came, and they filed in through the gates. I had seen no familiar face, nobody I could recognize. The inspector hadn't seen Dick Warren. He showed no disappointment.

"We came out early," he said, "but only just in case. I thought all along that anyone I'd want would be coming along later. Those were the people who wait from week to week and cry all the time they're waiting. They're the families and lovers and maybe friends. The ones who come up here on business don't stand around waiting for opening time. They can be eager to do business, but it's another kind of eagerness. It doesn't get them up early in the morning. It doesn't make them lose sleep."

We waited and people kept coming, but now they came by ones or twos and now the look was different. Whether the faces were furtive or assured, they had a recognizable toughness. Almost everyone who came was carrying a package or two, but these packages were as different as were the people. They had the look of something bought, the neatness of professional wrapping. They were just things money could buy.

Dick Warren came, and as he went through the gate, the inspector identified him for me. He looked much as I had expected he would look. He was expensively dressed without being well dressed. His jacket was too tight across the shoulders and too tight across the hips. They were big shoulders and heavy thighs, but good clothes would have accommodated to them. The face was expressionless, but not with that control that can wipe a face clean. This was vacuity.

I'm tempted to say it was a cruel face, but I suspect such judgments even when they are my own. Since Schmitty had filled me in on the man, I may well have been reading what I had been told into what I was seeing. He had a heavy jaw. It looked like a rock. All his features had a thick heaviness. In proportion, his eyes seemed too small. It may have been because they were so heavy lidded.

He went in the gate without ever looking our way, and the inspector made no move.

"Are you going in after him or are you going to pick him up on his way out?" I asked.

"Back in town," Schmitty said. "I'll find that one when I'm ready for him."

He didn't have to tell me that the ball was now in my court. We went on waiting and now I was the one who was doing all the watching. Visitors kept drifting in, but these ran to the Warren persuasion. They were showing no pain. When she came, I had an immediate recognition of her. She drove up to the gate and then went cruising slowly in search of a parking space. She was wearing a stormy look, but if anything, that might have been making recognition easier. The one time I had seen her she had been in a rage with the taxi driver. It occurred to me that ill temper might be the lady's permanent state of mind. I had the inspector alerted to her before she was parked.

"Are you sure?" he asked. "You want to be sure."

"I'm sure."

Watching her while she walked from her parking place to the gate and when she came past us on her way in, I had more than enough time for verification. I even had a recognition of the way she moved. It was the foot-stamping walk of an enraged woman. This was the woman I had seen. She was exactly as I remembered her and as the cabbie had described her. The inspector stood fast as she was going by us and he made no move for at least a quarter of an hour after that.

"Are you going to pick her up when she's on her way out?" I asked. "Or now that you've seen her, do you know where you can find her back in town?"

"Nobody I know," Schmitty said, "but since you're certain, that'll do for me."

It was not an answer to my question, but after that quarter of an hour and more I began to pick up on what the inspector had in mind. He headed back inside but only as far as the desk where they checked the visitors in. He looked at the sheet. I read it with him. It took no searching to find her name. It had to be the newest entry since in the fifteen minutes and more no further visitors had arrived.

"Jane Clark, 500 West 74th Street, New York, N.Y., to visit James Marshall."

"She keeps the fish tail well covered," Schmitty said.

Satisfied that he had all that he'd wanted in the prison, he headed back outside but not to pick up his car and return to town. I hadn't expected that he would be pulling out, so he had me baffled when he did go to his car and settle himself behind the wheel. I had a head full of questions when I got in beside him, but before I had sorted out what I would ask him first, he made the moves that gave me my answers. He pulled out of the place where he had been parked and moved to a spot from which he could get out quickly. It was also a spot that gave him an unimpeded view of the car Jane Clark had been driving.

"Hired car," he said. "It's a Z license plate."

"Lots of people in the city," I said, "don't own cars. They prefer to rent one whenever they need one. Garaging, parking, and insurance—it can work out cheaper. I've thought of doing it myself except that if you want one on short notice, you can't always be sure of getting one. Weekends, for instance, can be chancy."

"There's another advantage in a car hire," the inspector said. "If you're spotted in your own car, you're easier to trace."

I thought we might be in for a long wait, but much before I could have expected it, she was back out of the gate. The inspector switched on his ignition while he was watching her walk to her car.

"She wasn't with him long," I said. "Just about long enough to say 'mission accomplished.'"

"Not long enough to soothe her down and change her mood," the inspector said.

She was passing close enough to us to afford us a good

look at her face. It was at least as stormy as it had been earlier, and her walk again was carrying that suggestion of foot-stamping. What we were seeing was tantrum on the hoof.

She flung herself into the rented car and shot it out of its parking space. Her driving also carried the suggestion that she might be out of control.

Inspector Schmidt let her build a reasonable lead before he picked up the tail. I braced myself for a wild ride. When required, the inspector does things with a motor car that are more than breathtaking. They are heart-stopping. The way that babe was driving was all of that and more. Keeping her in sight promised to be hairy.

It began that way, but for all its wildness I could see nothing in it that would have indicated that she was aware that we were following along in her wake. However insane her driving, it had none of the characteristics that could be put down to evasive action.

I was further confirmed in that impression as we followed on down toward the city. By gradual stages she lowered her speed and did less and less of that dangerous zipping in and out of lanes. Long before we'd reached even the upper fringes of the Bronx she was driving soberly and safely. I breathed a sigh of relief.

Inspector Schmidt laughed. "She's worked herself out of her snit," he said.

Even in the city traffic she attempted none of the tricks you might expect from a driver who is trying to shake a tail. She made none of those sudden quick turns, no dashes across intersections in the face of changing lights. We came into the city on the West Side. When we were down into the Seventies, I remembered her address.

"Seventy-fourth coming up," I said. "Do we watch her park outside Five hundred West?"

"We watch her park," the inspector said.

That feat we were not to see accomplished. She went on by Seventy-fourth Street and at Seventy-second turned east. She drove into the park at the Seventy-second Street entrance, turning east and south on the winding Central Park road. At Fifty-ninth and Fifth she left the park and continued going east. When she parked, it was in the East Fifties in a stretch that was blocks away from anything residential.

Parking isn't permitted in that central area of the city. If you park there, you'll be towed away. Sometimes, if you're back to your car before any traffic officer has been by or before the tow truck gets around to you, you can get away with it. You are, nevertheless, always at risk.

Schmitty pulled in at the curb nearby. The traffic officers know Inspector Schmidt's car. Inspector Schmidt is never subjected to the inconvenience of being towed away. Our quarry took off on foot and we followed on foot. She turned up the avenue and did some languid window shopping as she went. She was showing not even a small residue of her earlier anger.

The avenue carries heavy traffic both on wheels and on foot. We kept our pace measured to hers, holding close enough so that we wouldn't lose her in the crowd but sufficiently screened from her by people to make it a likelihood that she wouldn't realize that she was being followed.

There's a big department store on the avenue. She walked around it, surveying the fashions displayed in the show windows, and then she doubled back to the store entrance and went in. We followed.

You'd have to know that store. Some time back they had the place done over and what they did to it is the last word. If it isn't the last word and any storekeeper comes up with anything more dizzying, it will be to lose all their customers to the funny factories.

The general lighting is dim except on the showcase counters where it is brilliant and concentrated. Every vertical flat surface is covered with mirror glass and the ceiling is also mirror-glass covered. Anywhere you look, you are confronted with your own image endlessly repeated down the receding planes of a limitless vista. Plunge into the place and you are immediately disoriented, never quite certain of what you see before you. It might be an entrance into the next selling area or it might be a mirror-coated dead end.

Why all of this should be a resounding success defies my understanding. I had long since concluded that I would never be able to come to comfortable terms with it, and I had been doing all my shopping elsewhere. I may, however, be alone in my susceptibility to the confusion. Other people apparently can take it without coming down with either headache or a feeling of queasiness. The place is always crowded, and that day was no exception.

Our mermaid—Inspector Schmidt, distrustful of her name, had taken to calling her that—moved into the crowded aisles and we lost her. I know of only one way I can explain it. At some point, confusing one of her many mirror-images with her, we walked into a looking glass. When we turned about to set ourselves straight, she was gone.

"Do you think we can find our way out of this?" Schmitty asked.

"Previous times I've been here," I said, "I've frothed at the mouth and they've taken me out."

"I'm not waiting for that," Schmitty said.

"It won't be long to wait."

We worked our way back to the entrance and came out into the traffic-clogged avenue where the madness has the virtue of not being diabolically calculated. I stopped to light a cigarette. The inspector was stopping for nothing. He took off at the fastest pace the crowded pavement permitted him. I pushed through the crowds to catch up with him.

"Where to now?" I asked.

"We'll wait for her to come back to her car."

# CHAPTER 9

We waited. Lunch time came and went and then it was
long gone. We had made that early start for the drive
upriver, and I was past the place where breakfast had been
even a dim memory.

"A man can starve," I said. "By the time she turns up,
we'll be so enfeebled by malnutrition that we won't be able
to cope with her."

"If she can take it, we can," the inspector said.

"There are restaurants in that store," I said. "Also it's a
well-known physiological fact that women have greater
reserves of body fat than men. Anyhow, on women shopping acts like a drug. They don't get hungry."

"Tailing acts like a drug on me," the inspector said.

"I don't drug. I'll go find a place that makes sandwiches.
I'll bring them back."

"Okay. If she turns up before you're back and I have to
take off, you go on home, eat your sandwiches and mine
too, and wait for me. I'll call you there."

I was torn between hunger and not wanting to miss anything. Hunger won hands down. When I returned with the
sandwiches, the rented car was still at the curb and the inspector was still waiting.

"I'm learning something," I said. "You can park a long
time before they tow you away."

"Don't you believe it. The tow truck's been by. I told them to leave her."

"How long?" I asked.

"Till she comes back, if she comes back."

"Shopping, she can take the whole day. She goes up to visit Marshall. She's spitting mad. What's she mad about? She's collected for services rendered and she got less than she thought she was worth. So then what's for her to do? She can go to her union and put in a complaint, or she can calm herself by going on a shopping spree and spending what she did get. After all, if she's not going back to the apartment, she has a lot of shopping to do, all those abandoned clothes to replace."

"She may be on a shopping spree," Schmitty said between bites of sandwich, "but the rest of that is garbage. She went up there mad. Anyhow the payoff wouldn't be made up there. Prisoners can have pocket money, but it isn't all that much. It won't be nearly enough to pay off a gal for setting a man up for murder, not nearly enough even if she is being fobbed off with something that's way under scale."

We sat in the car while the afternoon wound away. For the inspector it wasn't all idle time. He had his car telephone and he was keeping in touch with whatever was coming through for him down at headquarters. He was also putting out orders. He wanted a report on where Dick Warren was living and where he was hanging out. He also wanted a man sent up to where we were waiting. He had something he wanted picked up and put into process.

I was curious about that. So far as I knew he had nothing with him that he could want processed. I asked him. He brought out of his pocket a beautiful, clear snapshot. It was a Polaroid shot, one of those things that comes oozing out of the camera seconds after you've snapped it.

"The mermaid," he said. "Our photographers should do that good with the mug shots."

He wasn't exaggerating. He had me gasping.

"Where did you get that?" I asked.

"Snapped it outside the gate when she came by us. You weren't taking your eyes off her. You were paying no attention to me."

"So if she has a record . . ." I said.

"Even if she hasn't. A mermaid keeping the company she keeps, there can't be many of her. If there isn't a man on the force who knows her, somebody will have an informant who does."

The man came up from headquarters and went off with the snap and still we were waiting. Traffic along the avenue remained heavy. Since it had come to be going-home time, it had become, if anything, heavier than before. That, however, was the stuff that moved on wheels. The pedestrian traffic was thinning out. The inspector looked at his watch.

"It's past closing time," he said, "and dames don't shop in closed stores. That's another advantage of a rental car. You can walk away from it and no loss. That way it's not as good as a stolen car, but it's good enough."

"She knew we had a tail on her," I said.

"Sure enough looks like it," the inspector said. "That tells us something else about her. It's encouraging. The lady's a pro. That business the night you saw her had me a little worried. I was afraid that maybe she wasn't and then she could be hard to find."

"That business baffles me," I said. "What she did that night."

"In the light of her expert performance today, I think I'm beginning to have that figured."

"In the light of her performance today, I find it impossible to figure."

"You have to put it together with her going to visit Marshall and going there mad and coming away mad."

I tried putting it together, but all I came up with was a lot of jagged contours that could never be joined. We left the rental car for the tow-away truck and headed uptown. Up in Yorkville we passed the carpentry shop. It was lighted and we could see Cal Williams at work inside. He kept long hours. We didn't stop. Our destination was the hide-away hotel room and Froman.

We found him lying down with a damp towel over his eyes. His bodyguard was sitting beside him and reading a newspaper.

"What's the matter with him?" the inspector asked.

"Nothing. He's just resting his eyes. He said he was going blind looking at the pictures. He says he's coming down with pros poisoning."

"That you don't get from just looking. Has he hit the book I had sent up?"

Froman lifted the towel off one eye. It was his better eye and it regarded the inspector balefully.

"I've been looking and looking and looking," he said. "I earned a little rest."

"You didn't find her?"

"No, I didn't find her. I kept hoping I would. I kept hoping I could stop before I'd had to go through the whole blasted lot of them, but no such luck. She isn't there."

"I sent up some more. I'm looking for you to have better luck with the new ones."

Groaning, Froman rose to sitting position. "All right," he said. "I might as well get it over with."

The inspector opened the book and set it on the table. Froman pulled up a chair.

"I want you to study these carefully," the inspector said.

Froman looked at the first of the lot and moved to shove his chair back.

"These are men," he said. "What can I find here?"

"A variety of things," the inspector told him. "Maybe you'll spot her twin brother. Maybe you'll spot a man or men you've been seeing in P.J.'s. Maybe you'll come on the guys who beat on you."

"Guy," Froman said. "Only one guy."

"You've been saying two."

"That was when I was trying to make you believe it was a mugging. It was only one man. He told me to say I was mugged and by two men."

"One man. Then look for him."

With the three of us, the inspector, Froman's bodyguard, and me standing over him, Froman began turning the pages. We were watching him as he did it. After a couple of moments the inspector stopped him.

"You're going too fast," he said. "I want you studying them."

He flipped the pages back to the beginning and Froman began again. This time he gave the pictures more study. He was going through them at an even studious pace until he came to one I recognized. It was Dick Warren. He gave that one no more than a quick glance before he flipped over to the next. That one also got no more than the quick glance. He was back to his old pace. The inspector stopped him once more.

"You're rushing it again," he said, as he turned the pages back to Warren's picture. "Take a good look. Study them."

Froman squirmed. He sighed.

"Yes, Inspector," he said. "That one."

"Twin brother?"

"No." He indicated his eye and his lip. "That's the man who gave me these."

"Good," the inspector said. "I had no way of knowing whether he gave them to you or he ordered them up for you. Since he did the job himself, it simplifies things for us. In that department we don't have to look for anyone else."

Froman started to rise. The inspector pushed him back into his chair.

"That's great for starters, but you're still looking for the twin brother and for any men you may have seen hanging out in P.J.'s."

Froman sighed and moaned and mumbled inarticulate protests, but with Inspector Schmidt standing over him he went through the whole lot with every evidence of giving them the attention the inspector was demanding. When he had been through the whole volume and had carefully scrutinized every picture, the inspector let him come away from it.

Froman went back to lying down with the damp towel over his eyes. His swellings had gone down considerably and he was coming back to looking himself again. I had a hunch that his damp towel routine was a device for being alone with his resentments. It was that or, as it had been with Jacques, it was an ostrich-like hiding place.

Schmitty offered Froman a comforting word. "It won't be much longer," he said. "With any luck I might even have this all wrapped up tonight."

"You mean you're going to arrest that man and it'll be safe for me to go home again?"

"Briefly if you want to," the inspector said.

"What does briefly mean?"

"It means that I'll have the whole bunch of them under arrest and you'll be safe until they've made bail. Then you'll need protection again until they have come to trial and you have testified. Once your sworn testimony has gone before a jury, you'll be safe. There will be no profit to them in silencing you then. You will have spoken. Touching you then will be nothing to gain and much to lose. They're practical men. They don't make things worse for themselves without purpose."

"Till they come to trial and I have testified, how long will that be?"

It was Inspector Schmidt's turn to sigh. "I'm sorry about that," he said. "It's likely to be a long time—too long. Crowded court calendars, motions for postponement. Do I have to tell you?"

"But my office?"

"Can you handle it by telephone? Papers sent to you here. Conferences, if necessary, here. Of course, we'll have to screen the people."

Froman grimaced. "Yes," he said. "I suppose so since I'm stuck with it, but it's a hell of a note. Do you realize that what it amounts to is that they'll be walking around free out on bail and I'm the one who'll be locked up?"

"I realize it. The DA will make a pitch for denying them bail. He'll try to convince the judge that they're too much a menace to be left loose."

"That's not what you said before."

"I didn't want to hand you any false hopes. Sure, the DA

will make his pitch, but I can't promise you that he'll suc-
ceed. Judges don't often deny bail. Judges are kind of
remote from the streets. They look the other way, toward
how the higher courts will take what they do, and those
judges on the higher courts, they're even more remote from
the streets. I'm sorry."

"You're sorry." Froman was an embittered man, a ripe
candidate for the Moral Majority.

We left him. Schmitty took the volumes of pictures with
him. The two of us went down to the car heavy laden.

"I'd like to use your place tonight," he said.

*"Mi casa es su casa,"* I said.

"Be yourself, *Jorge,*" the inspector said.

"You're living in an increasingly bilingual city. Keep up
with the times."

"I called you Jorge, didn't I?"

"So you did."

He drove around to the neighborhood but, when he
pulled up, it was in front of the atelier. Jacques had shut
down for the night, but the shop wasn't dark. Rudy was in
there cleaning the place up. The inspector tapped on the
glass panel of the door. Rudy had his back to us. Without
turning to look, he dove behind the shop's reception desk.
The inspector tapped some more. Rudy popped up from
behind the desk, but now he had a gun in his hand. He lev-
eled it in the direction of the door. The inspector always
carries a small flashlight in his pocket. He brought it out
and shone the beam up on our faces. Rudy relaxed and set
the gun down on the desk. He was all apologies when he
had unlocked the door.

"Holdups," he said. "Too many holdups. I don't open for
nobody when it's like this, everybody gone for the night."

"We're not sticking you up," Schmitty said.

"I know. You're Inspector Schmidt. I know, but there's nobody here, nobody but me."

"That's all right. It's you I want."

"What for?"

"Just to look at some pictures."

"I'm almost through here."

"How long?"

"Ten minutes, maybe fifteen."

The inspector was satisfied with that. He told Rudy to come around to my place as soon as he'd locked up. He gave him the address.

"We'll get dinner sent in," Schmitty told him. "The three of us can eat, and you'll look at the pictures for me."

There's a local restaurant—not P.J.'s. It's a good little place and they'll send out casseroles and stuff. We use them often, the inspector and I. We stopped in there and the inspector spread himself. He was ordering for three and he went all out. Rudy was going to have the feed of his life. I suppose Schmitty was also making it up to me for lunch.

Rudy was as good as his word. In exactly fifteen minutes he was at my door. I could have wished that he had been less prompt. I wanted a drink, but the inspector had warned me against offering Rudy any.

"Not until he's done his job on the mug shots," he said. "After that the lid's off."

Since Schmitty had used up most of the fifteen minutes making his order in the restaurant, I hadn't had time for even a quick one. Then I could hardly break out the whiskey without pouring some for our guest.

The inspector set him right down to his job, starting him with the women. Nobody had to slow Rudy up. He gave each shot long and absorbed scrutiny. He could have been confronting a great sheaf of *Playboy* centerfolds. The food arrived and Rudy went on with the pictures while he ate. Absorbed in what he appeared to be taking as a bevy of beauties, he was doing his eating mechanically. It was, nonetheless, an efficient machine. Divided attention didn't keep him from stowing away the food at a great rate.

Although he lingered longer over some of the pictures than over the others, it was never with any sign of recognition. It was merely a matter of degree of enjoyment. The luscious babes held him longer than the spare types. It was not unlikely that Rudy was a man surfeited with his daylong, daily confrontations with the fashionably thin females that made up the atelier's feminine clientele. He was still engrossed with the hookers when we had finished dinner. He knew he was looking for the big redhead. He kept assuring the inspector that he would know her when he saw her.

"I won't have to study on that one," he said again and again. "I'll know her like a shot."

Eventually he had seen the last of them and with obvious regret he set them aside.

"You have some nice ones there," he said. "There's a lot there I could go for, but not her. She ain't there."

Inspector Schmidt turned him to the men.

"Guys?" Rudy said. "I ain't seen no guys without it was him, he got himself bumped off."

"You may have seen something you don't realize you've seen," the inspector said.

Rudy started, but now the inspector had to stand over him and keep slowing him down. Guys, even though among what he was seeing were some spectacularly pretty ones, did nothing for Rudy. With Inspector Schmidt keeping him to the required pace, he was going methodically through them, but that was just paying for his dinner. Rudy was bored.

He hadn't gone halfway through that set when one of the inspector's boys came up from headquarters. He had with him the mermaid shot Schmitty had sent down there. Before listening to what the man had to report, the inspector took the snap and set it down before Rudy.

Rudy blinked. "That's her," he said. "Not the one you're looking for, not that one. That's Miss Smith."

"Mary Smith?"

"Yeah, her. The third-floor-rear. Him, the one got his self killed, he was her boyfriend. That's her looking like she's going to bite somebody's head off."

"I forgot to tell her to say 'cheese,'" the inspector said. "Go on with the men."

Leaving Rudy at it, we took the man from headquarters out to the kitchen.

"Vice squad knows her," the man said, "but they don't have her as Mary Smith, Inspector."

"She's not the first Mary Smith who isn't Mary Smith," Schmitty said. "The name smelled right from the beginning."

"They know her as Margaret Warren," the man said, "maiden name—Margaret Dalton. Some time back she was married or maybe not married but just living with the guy. They haven't been together now for a couple, three years. Vice has it that she left town. If she's back, they don't know it."

"What's on Warren?" Schmitty asked.

"Done time on assault. He used to belong to Jim Marshall. Could be he still does."

"Dick Warren," the inspector said. "He still belongs to Marshall."

"Want a work-up on him, Inspector?"

"I've been asking what we've got on him. I asked for current address and where he hangs out."

"I'll get it for you, Inspector."

"Nobody told you I asked?"

"No, Inspector."

"What goes on with you guys? Aren't you talking to each other any more?"

"I've been on the dame, Inspector. I've been over with the guys in Vice. I haven't talked to anybody else."

"Never mind then. The boys will be working on it. They'll get it to me."

"When I get back downtown, I'll light a fire under them."

"You do that," Schmitty said. "Margaret Dalton—Margaret Warren—what does Vice have on her? Hooker?"

"Maybe once, but if she was, it'll be before they ever had any line on her. They could never get anything nailed down, but they had her pegged for an importer."

"Importer" meant nothing to me, or in any event I knew that such meaning as it did have couldn't have been germane to the topic in hand.

"Western meat?" Inspector Schmidt asked.

"Brings them in and gets them set up with a pimp."

"Teenage Minnesota farm girls," I said.

They had explored it far enough to get me tuned in. I knew about those blocks along Eighth Avenue in the Forties known to the Vice Squad as the Minnesota Strip.

"And Sterling came back from Minnesota exile," the inspector said. "The Feds when they tucked him away should have been talking to the Vice Squad. They maybe picked the wrong part of the country for him."

We returned to Rudy. Instead of working on the stuff

we'd left him, he had switched back to the pictures he pre-
ferred. He might have been choosing the ones he would
take home with him for pin-ups. Inspector Schmidt spoiled
his fun. He gathered together all the shots of the hookers
and loaded them onto his man to take back to headquarters.

"We're through with these," he said.

With a sorrowful gaze Rudy watched them go out the
door. The inspector started him through the remaining pictures again. With the inspector there to keep him slowed
down, he gave every one of the shots serious attention. He
was more than halfway through when he turned up a picture that lifted him out of his mood of pained boredom. He
looked at it a long time. Then he shut his eyes for a few
moments and looked again.

"It's hard to tell for sure," he said.

"You think you know this one?" Schmitty asked.

"Not for sure," Rudy repeated, "but it just could be."

"In a red wig and women's clothes?"

"That's what I'm thinking," Rudy said. "If it ain't, it's
got to be it's her brother."

The inspector turned the picture over. I crowded in. I
was with him for reading the information on the back. It
was all there. Transvestite. There was no homicide record,
but there were a couple of assaults and some robberies.
Alone with a man in a hotel room, he would beat his sex
partner unconscious and then rob him. Any man who
made the mistake of taking him home would also be running a heavy risk of being beaten unconscious and waking
up to find his lover gone and gone with him anything of
value that might have been in the house.

This was no unique pattern. For all too many gays it's a
built-in risk. Need obliterates caution. Also a man who

might sheer off from too tough-looking a character might be taken by that same character in drag.

His name was Gus Rogers. They had him down as a.k.a. Augusta Rogers and Gussie Rogers.

I remembered that early on the inspector had considered the possibility of a wig and drag, but when he'd had Froman look for a twin brother, I hadn't made the connection.

"From what it says here, he'd done it before. It may have been his regular thing."

"Getting into drag?" the inspector said. "Being his regular thing doesn't take much away from its value as a disguise. Froman didn't see through it."

"I'm wondering," I said, "if he didn't or he didn't want to."

"He didn't. Rudy, here, has had experience. He has an educated eye. He works in the hairdresser's shop. Wigs don't fool him. In the shop he's seeing it all the time— women putting them on and women taking them off. He's alive to the ways a wig can change a person's appearance. With all this unisex crap going, he may even have seen guys try on women's wigs."

"No," Rudy was quick to say, "they come in for a trim or to get theirselves styled. They's some they get fitted for a rug or just a little hairpiece to fill in where it's bare, but we don't get none they want a woman's wig. It's only sometimes one of the operators—he's restyling a dame's wig— he may put it on himself to check on how it's coming along. I seen that sometimes."

"Our friend has earned a drink," Schmitty said.

"Don't mind if I do," Rudy said.

Since I was long past where I could have minded, I fixed

one for Rudy and one for myself. I offered the inspector one, but he turned me down.

"When I'm ready to pack it in for the night," he said.

I did him a straight Bitter Lemon and, while we were working on the drinks, he talked to Rudy. He told him he'd done a great job.

"As soon as I have him," he said, "I'll be taking you downtown to identify him. That should be pretty soon. Later you'll have to do it again in court before a jury and under oath."

Rudy suffered none of the qualms that had afflicted Froman. He showed every indication of looking forward to a couple of promised treats. It was probably the first time in the man's life that he had ever felt important. He was looking forward to some delightful breaks from sweeping hair off the barber shop floor.

We finished our drinks and Rudy happily agreed to a second. For him this was going to be a night to remember. The inspector waited till he had put himself outside that one, and then he turned Rudy loose. While we were drinking there had been a phone call. It was for the inspector. He had taken it in another room and coming back from the phone he urged Rudy to drink up.

"Warren," he said, after I had seen Rudy to the door. "He's operating down in the Village. Lives on Jones Street, and he hangs out in a joint on Sheridan Square. It's called The Snortery. Know it?"

"Never even heard of it," I said. "I don't go for the joints with the cutesy names."

"P.J.'s?"

"Proximity. It's the nearest watering hole."

"The Snortery belongs to a man named Abe Link. The dope is that Link is a front for Warren."

"Who is a front for Jim Marshall."

"Not unlikely, but there's nothing to say that Warren can't be having some little operation of his own with Marshall's blessing."

"I hope Link isn't short for Lincoln," I said.

"Don't put it past him," Schmitty said. "He's been called Honest Abe. It's always a good bet that a guy who's called Honest Anything just isn't."

"Abraham Lincoln was."

"There's always an exception, and anyhow he wasn't in the nightclub business."

"Taking Warren tonight?" I asked.

"We'll talk to him, but for now I'll want to leave him on the loose to lead us to Mrs. Warren. I'd like to get to her before she gets over being mad."

"Funny she should be Mrs. Warren."

"Nothing new about keeping things in the family," Schmitty said.

"I was thinking that George Bernard Shaw would have liked it."

"How does he get into the act?"

"He wrote a play called *Mrs. Warren's Profession.*"

"The right profession?"

"Yes."

The inspector climbed into his shoes and we headed down to the Village.

"You going to try Froman again on that shot of Gus Rogers a.k.a. Augusta and Gussie?" I asked.

The inspector shook his head. "I'd rather have him go in for the line-up cold. The two of them, Rudy and Froman, I'll have them look at a line-up of guys in drag. I don't want anyone thinking I primed Froman on what to look for."

"You're going to pull in a flock of transvestites?"

"No. Four or five of the guys I have in Homicide will look real good in red wigs and shiny tight dresses."

"The guys are going to like that."

"All in a day's work. How about you? It would be something you could write about."

"No, thanks."

"Chicken."

"Not at all. I'll need to be in the audience so that I can see Froman and Rudy react at firsthand. Also the both of them know me. I'd be a familiar face. They might just pick me instead of Gussie and that would mess you up good and plenty."

"They couldn't pick you," Inspector Schmidt said. "You wouldn't look tough enough."

# CHAPTER 10

We tried the Jones Street address and drew something of a blank there. It was where Dick Warren was living, but there was nobody home. We moved on to Sheridan Square. The Snortery was so typical that it could have been any one of a dozen such joints. The Village is thick with them, but they are sprinkled over the rest of the city as well.

I am ready to bet that none of the neighborhood people ever went into the place. It was strictly for the yokels, and in the Village locals and yokels are like the proverbial oil and water. They may collide but they never collude. I wouldn't call it a tourist trap. It had neither the flash nor the size. It was small, and it had that dinginess that makes you look twice before you can believe that it isn't dirty.

The lighting was murky and the tables were small. Tables of that size are great promoters of drink-spilling. The more overpriced shots spilled, the more overpriced shots sold. There was a piano at the end of the bar and an entertainer. The piano was an ancient upright well past any time when it might have been tunable. As each note was struck, I found myself watching for a flock of moths to come flying out of the felts.

The entertainer was a wisp of a man with long strands of black hair carefully slicked across his baldness. The hair was startlingly black against the pallor of the pate that showed between the strands. The hair was black as no hair can ever be on its own. It didn't look dyed. It looked blackened. I could think only of shoe polish.

He worked the piano for a limp accompaniment to his singing. Musically his songs were nothing. The emphasis was on the lyrics and those were made up entirely from shopworn double entendres. His face was startling. It was much too old for its innocence of even the first wrinkle. It was the face of a baby who had lived too long. The face went with the songs. It was at once tired and puerile.

There were some people along the bar. They looked as though they had come over from Jersey City or Hackensack for a night on the town. The men were in double-knit suits that, whether gray or brown or blue, pushed color past the line of probability. The women were also encased in double-knits, but theirs showed constellations of spangles concentrated in the most unlikely places. The double-knit brigade was noisy. They laughed immoderately at the songs. They behaved as respectable people behave when they are taking a dip into deviltry.

Although the place wasn't full, it was doing good business, good enough so that there were only a few unoccupied tables. We took one of them. Back in the murkiest of the corners there was a couple that had me bemused. The woman had the look of a hooker, but it would have needed a lot of man to take her on. She was a big woman, big and heavy.

If she had been a redhead, I would have been thinking pay dirt, but she was a blonde with an absurd rosebud mouth and false eyelashes so long and thick and furry that on them alone she could have taken best of breed in a sheepdog show.

What had me marveling was the man. Some of the double-knits along the bar were stevedore types who could have entered the ring in her weight division, but the bird at the table with her was a little man. I couldn't see whether he was wearing a hearing aid, but he had the look that, for some reason I have never tried to analyze, always suggests hearing aids to me. He looked like a small-time accountant who had begun to come apart. It is the look of meticulousness and of uncertainty.

We had no more than taken the table, when Inspector Schmidt left me at it and took himself to a phone booth by the front door. While he was on the phone, a waiter came over to take my order. The service in these places is never good, but it is always quick. You are never left to sit around not producing revenue. If that waiter wasn't a fighter, he had been one. He had the heavy wrists and the facial scars you'll see around the training gyms.

I ordered two whiskies. This was not the kind of waiter who could be asked for a glass of Perrier with a twist of lime. In joints like The Snortery, if you want the booze to do more than wet the bottom of the glass, you have to order a double. I didn't order doubles. Even though Inspector Schmidt considered himself to be on duty, he could take what that waiter would bring and never call it drinking. On the other hand, if Schmitty was going to be technical, I could drink his for him.

He was back at the table when the waiter delivered the drinks. I didn't have to taste to know that they were as expected. The inspector had a question for the waiter.

"You got a back room here?" he asked.

"You want the Gents, it's by the door. Right by the phone booth. You was just now there. Ain't you seen it?"

"I seen it. I asked you about a back room."

"What's a matter? You don't like it out here?"

"That door?" Schmitty indicated a door behind the entertainer's piano bench. "Back room?"

"It ain't for no public," the waiter said, and went off across the room to swab a table top that probably needed no swabbing.

"Surly," I said.

"Not authorized to answer questions about back rooms," Schmitty said.

"If Warren is back there, won't he be alerted to slip out some rear door?"

"There is a rear door and I have it covered. If he uses it, he'll be tailed."

"That was your phone call?"

"My boys move fast but not that fast," Schmitty said. "The phone call I had up at your place. I set it up then. The boys are there. I saw them when we were on the way in."

So then we just sat there. I worked on my glass of faintly tinted water. The inspector took occasional sips out of his. We were doing nothing. It seemed to me a stupid exercise, perhaps designed to determine just how nervous Warren might be. I was telling myself that this was Inspector Schmidt and that Inspector Schmidt was not going to keep his shoes on for any stupid exercises, but nevertheless I kept wondering what he could have been building.

I was itching to ask him, but I had been in such situations before. I'd ask and it would only be to find that I had failed to think of something humiliatingly obvious. I kept silent and I tried to think. I got nowhere with it.

It was a good twenty minutes of this nothing. Then four men came in and took places at the bar. They were four I knew, and with their arrival the inspector moved. They were four good Homicide cops. I spend too much time with the inspector not to know the men on his squad. That had been his phone call and that had been the reason for the idle waiting. He had called in reinforcements, and he hadn't been moving until he had his troops in place.

That was good enough, but I still had my questions. It seemed too much marshaling of forces for the situation. He didn't know whether he was even going to find Dick Warren in that back room. Also he had told me that he wasn't planning on any immediate arrest. He wanted to leave Warren on the loose to lead him to Mary Smith.

He left the table and I followed him. There was no question about where he was going. If we weren't moving in a straight line for the inspector's objective, it was only because the route involved some twisting in and out to negotiate a passage between the tiny tables.

By the time we had circled the entertainer's piano bench, there was a man planted between us and the door to that room that wasn't for the public. Making the necessary stop, I had a close-up look at the entertainer's hair. Up close the black looked even more like shoe polish. I was noticing that, however, only in passing. The main event was coming on between Inspector Schmidt and the man who stood barring the door.

"Anything I can do for you, sir?" the man asked.

He was a pot-bellied little guy in a black suit and a black turtleneck shirt. He had his hands in his jacket pockets, and there was a little bulge that couldn't be hand. It was only a moment or two later, when he brought his hands out because he needed them for gesticulation that I saw that it wasn't a brass knuckle. It was a diamond ring of impressive dimensions. The man looked like an undertaker out of uniform.

"Who are you?" Inspector Schmidt asked.

"This is my place."

"Abe Link?"

"That's me. I don't know who you are."

"Inspector Schmidt. Police."

"What can I do for you, Inspector?"

"For me you can step aside," Schmitty said. "For yourself you can keep out of something that can't do you any good."

"Look, Inspector. There's nothing in there. It's my office. It's got my desk and it's got my books. The IRS comes in and looks at my books. The Alcohol Board comes in and looks at my books. You want to look at my books?"

"Step aside."

"You got a warrant?"

"I can get one, but meanwhile I have four men here. You can see them over there at the bar. I have more men on your back door. Your customers will be free to come and go, but nobody I want will leave here except under escort and with cuffs on him."

"Inspector, there's nobody here you want."

"Then you and I can have a little talk in your office. I promise I won't touch your books, but if you are at all smart, you know you can be closed up without anyone looking at your books."

"Look, Inspector." The little man was beginning to sweat. "I'm a little guy I got a little business. You ask anybody and they'll tell you Link is straight, straight as a die. Couldn't you just go away and do this someplace else? Like I told you, my name's Link. You're going to fix it so I'll be the missing link."

Through none of this had he been loud. It had all been done at a level that couldn't disturb the customers, but that last speech was pleading, and for that he had dropped his voice to an only barely audible level. His little pun was pathetic. He couldn't have been hoping that he could divert the inspector with humor, but he was trying.

At that moment the door opened behind him. Dick Warren opened it. It was a good guess that he had been listening through the door. When the level had dropped to where he couldn't hear it, inevitably it had worried him.

"This guy giving you trouble, Abe?" he said.

It was Dick Warren to the rescue. Nobody could push his little friend, Abe Link, around.

In a breathless rush, Link worked at setting him right. He was so anxious to get the words out quickly that he had syllables tumbling one over the other.

"Police," he said. "Inspector Schmidt. Police Inspector."

I'm not going to attempt to reproduce the garble he gave out. It seemed impossible that Warren could have understood it unless he'd had the basis of what he'd heard through the door for untangling it.

"What have you against this good man, Inspector?" Warren asked.

"Nothing much," the inspector said. "Nothing more than his unwillingness to let me speak to you."

"Your business is with me, Inspector? Don't blame Abe. You see, I have a lady in here. It's all right, but I guess Abe was afraid it might be compromising. Come in, gentlemen."

He did have a lady with him. She was his former wife or possibly his former cohabitant. The police records had been vague on that point.

"Miss Smith," the inspector said.

"Mrs. Warren." She couldn't have been cooler or more composed.

"Jane Clark," the inspector said.

"Margaret Warren."

"Five hundred West Seventy-fourth Street. I'm glad to see that you've come up out of the wet."

Warren stepped between them.

"What do you want, Inspector?" he asked.

He acted as though he were taking over. He had shut the door behind us, shutting Link out.

"I want you," the inspector said. "I want the lady. I'll want Jim Marshall, but for now he's all right where he is."

"You're making a mistake, Inspector," Warren said. "It's a natural mistake. I can understand your making it, but still you are mistaken."

"You're ready to cooperate and set me straight?"

"Have I a choice?"

The question was asked lightly. Warren couldn't have been cooler or more self-assured.

"You haven't," Schmitty said.

"It's about Jack Sterling, isn't it?"

"What else?"

"I just wanted to be sure we were talking about the same thing."

"We're talking about the same thing."

"You know Ole Jensen," Warren said. "He calls himself Paddy."

"It's not an alias. He's Paddy for legitimate business reasons."

"I know that. He's a good man, but he has a cousin."

"Cal Williams," the inspector said.

"You know? Then why do I have to tell you?"

"Because you have no choice," the inspector said.

"Sterling made the mistake of hanging out in Ole Jensen's place. Jensen recognized him and passed the word to his cousin. Williams never had good business sense. A businessman knows that what's done is done. You cut your losses and go on to something else. It's no good going back to what can't be helped anymore. All you do is start up again the thing that has been finished and that you want to keep finished."

"Williams didn't kill Jack Sterling."

"If he didn't, Inspector, then he had it done."

"What about your part in it?" the inspector asked.

"Me, Inspector? I had no part in it. I'm a businessman, and I've just been telling you. In business we don't open up what's better left closed."

"It's good business practice," the inspector said, "but you let it slip your mind. I have two witnesses who will identify the killer. You knew about one of them. You assaulted him and threatened him. He'll identify you. He's afraid to do it, but you can't count on that because I've convinced him that he has to be more afraid of not doing it."

Warren switched over to a rueful look. The lady seemed unconcerned, as though she were no more than an interested observer. She could have been preparing to go into competition with me in writing an account of the case. So far as anything in her demeanor might have been speaking for what she had in mind, her interest would have been about at that level.

"Yes," Warren admitted, but almost cheerfully, "I did make that mistake."

"How did you come to do it since it was contrary to your sound business methods?" the inspector asked.

His tone wasn't inquisitorial. He sounded merely curious.

"A favor for a friend," Warren said. "Paddy made the

mistake of telling Cal that Jack Sterling was back in town. Paddy isn't too bright. It never occurred to him that Cal would go ape. If he had asked me, I could have told him; but before I knew anything about it, it was done. I couldn't care less about Cal Williams. If he was so stupid, he could stew in his own juice, but he had put poor, dumb Paddy on the spot. I tried to help Paddy. It was a mistake. You don't let sentiment interfere with business, but a man's only human. We all have those times when we go soft."

"Soft" seemed hardly the word for what he had done to Froman, but he wasn't telling a bad story. Juries have been known to go for such stories.

The inspector turned to the lady. "Jack Sterling was killed in your apartment," he said.

"I have Williams to thank for that. It didn't just happen that it was there. It was intentional, and the way you've come in here, Inspector, it seems as though it's worked. Cal expected that if it was done up in my place, it would lead you to Dick."

"That," the inspector said, "can work both ways. You people expected that with the thing hooked into P.J.'s, I'd be led to Cal Williams."

Warren picked up on that. "Oh, come on, Inspector!" he said. "You can't think we're that stupid. We have the guy bumped and we stage it so it'll finger us?"

"Things go wrong."

"That wrong? We don't let things go that wrong."

Again the inspector switched it over to the lady.

"You brought Sterling back to town," he said.

"If you want to put it that way, Inspector. He was a big boy. He came back to town."

"With you. To hole up in your apartment."

"He wanted to come. He was bored out West. He had

nothing going for him out there. He was only existing. Also, if you must know, we were in love."

"You and Jack Sterling? Aren't you the wrong sex?"

"Jack was a complicated man, Inspector. He loved me and I loved him, but he also had needs I couldn't satisfy. I understood that, and I accepted it."

"And your husband?"

"I have no husband."

"Mrs. Warren has no husband?"

"Dick and I broke up years ago. It was an amicable breakup. We've never stopped being friends."

It was in the best contemporary style, cool, and intelligent.

"You were in love," the inspector said. "Sterling wanted to come back so that he could be with you. For just one night?"

"Love is not only the nights, Inspector. It is days as well. There were to be other days and nights. We expected a long future of them."

"For the brief times you would be in town and between the times when he would be satisfying his other needs?"

"I was quitting the traveling."

"But one night and you changed your mind?"

"One last trip, Inspector, to close things down."

"How long were you thinking you were going to have before Jack Sterling's past would be catching up with him?" the inspector asked.

"I wouldn't have let him come East if I had known there was any danger. I had every assurance that nobody would be out to get him. I didn't know about this Cal Williams. Nobody knew that he would be anyone to worry about."

"Sterling was worried. He holed up in the apartment and he wasn't opening the door to anyone."

"Just on the surface of things you know that's not true, Inspector. The way his death was reported, he wasn't killed through a closed door."

"When people came to the door, he let nobody in. He made the mistake of bringing someone in. The one person he trusted was the wrong one."

"It was emotional, Inspector. After years of hiding away it was going to take time before he could feel safe. I told him there was no need for it and he believed me, but hiding had become a habit. Of course, I was wrong, but I had no way of knowing I was wrong."

"The one night you were with him, you took him to P.J.'s for dinner. After you left, he broke the hiding habit every night to go hang out in P.J.'s. Did you know he was going to do that?"

"I expected he would. I was going to be away. He would go crazy alone in the apartment, seeing nobody, talking to nobody. I got him to go out with me that night. I wanted to show him that he would be all right. If he was afraid, he didn't have to go out of the neighborhood. The neighborhood was safe."

"And you picked P.J.'s, the one place in the neighborhood that was unsafe?"

"That was bad luck. He was nervous out in the street. P.J.'s is the closest place. From the apartment to P.J.'s he was hardly out in the street at all. Of course, if I had known about Williams and that Paddy was his cousin, I would have given up the apartment and moved way off to some other part of town before I let him come East with me. That is if I would have let him come East at all. I certainly would never have taken him to P.J.'s."

"You told him he would be safe there?"

"I thought he would be safe anywhere, and I told him he

would be. It was going to take time before he could have come around to feeling that way. I tried to get him to feel there was at least one place he could go and feel safe. I didn't want him going out of his mind in the few days I was going to be away. I picked the worst possible place. That was my bad luck."

"What about his bad luck?"

"We were in love, Inspector. His bad luck was my bad luck."

"You knew he would be spending all his evenings there?"

"I thought he would be going there for his meals. I would have liked to have hoped that he would gain enough confidence to go other places as well, but it seems he didn't."

"You were in love with him, but when you got back to the apartment and saw police around, you had no interest in knowing what was happening to the man you loved. You took off and made yourself hard to find. Why?"

"I couldn't imagine that he had been killed. I thought he was in some kind of trouble, and if I could stay loose, I'd be in a better position to help him."

"When you saw the TV news and read the papers, you were still going to help him?"

"I knew what you people would be thinking. I know the conclusions you jump to."

"Jane Clark visited Jim Marshall regularly for several weeks," the inspector said. "Why was it Jane Clark and not Margaret Warren or Mary Smith?"

It was a question I expected would give her trouble, but she was ready for it. She had wanted to bring her lover back to New York, but she was not going to do it unless she was convinced she could do it without any danger to

Sterling. It had taken several visits to Marshall before she could be satisfied that she had complete assurance. At the same time she didn't want anyone thinking that he was coming back as Marshall's man, since he wasn't. Therefore, she had been Jane Clark.

"You weren't easily persuaded," the inspector said.

She insisted it wasn't that. It had only been that she had to be sure. She kept going back to check with Marshall. It hadn't been till he had been able to assure her that he had contacted everybody and that everybody understood and was agreed that Jack Sterling was to be left alone, that Marshall wanted nothing done to him, that she had been ready to let Sterling come back East.

"Marshall knew about Cal Williams," the inspector said.

"And he misjudged him. It has to be that he misjudged him. Marshall's no fool. He knows that this is not likely to do him any good the next time he comes up for parole."

"Jane Clark's visit today?" the inspector asked.

"I was furious."

"You were. I could see that, but you were thinking it was just a misjudgment. You don't allow a man a misjudgment? As Dick said, we're all human."

"Not knowing about Williams and Paddy, I didn't understand that it was a misjudgment. I was thinking that Jim Marshall had played a double game with me. He let me bring Jack back East, and then he had him killed in my apartment so that all the suspicion could fall on me."

"And you don't think that anymore?"

"Now that I know about Williams and Paddy, I can see how it had to be. Marshall made an understandable mistake. After that it was just bad luck."

"He knew about Williams even if he did misjudge him, and he knew where you were living and where you would be taking Sterling. Don't you think he might have warned you about Paddy just in case?"

"He didn't know they were cousins. Nobody knew they were cousins until afterward."

"So Jim Marshall explained everything today and you were satisfied that he had nothing to do with Sterling's murder. All the same, you were still furious when you left him."

"Of course, I was. I was furious with Williams and with Paddy. What they had done to me—shouldn't I have been angry?"

The inspector doubled back. "You say nobody knew Paddy and Cal Williams were cousins. That's not what Paddy tells me." Schmitty turned to Warren. "He tells me that you knew. He tells me that for five years he's been paying you protection with the added incentive of keeping you quiet about his relationship with his jailbird cousin."

Warren shrugged. "When a guy's desperate, when he's trying to save his own skin, he'll say anything. It's what I get for doing favors."

"Only the beginning of what you get," the inspector said. "I'm taking you in, the both of you. I'm charging you with complicity in the murder of Jack Sterling. You can pray that a jury will like your story better than I do."

The lady started to protest. Warren just picked up the phone and dialed. In the few moments he was waiting to be put through, he soothed her down.

"I'm calling my lawyer," he said. "We'll be out almost before we are in. He can't hold us. He has nothing. A little assault charge on me maybe, but that's all—nothing on you."

He made his call. The inspector opened the back door. The men he had stationed out there came in and put the cuffs on the two prisoners. They were about to take them out that back door when uproar broke out in the barroom. Have you ever heard a shrill baritone? It's hardly a common phenomenon. I'm certain it was the first time for me. The inspector had his men change course. We were going out the front way and taking the Warrens with us.

It was screaming and cursing out there and a full range of obscenities, all the run-of-the-mill words plus some rarities that must rate as museum pieces. They were coming out of the rosebud mouth of the big blonde.

The small-time accountant type who'd been at the table with her was still with her and not only in his person but with his vocabulary as well. His range was quite the equal of hers. They had tried to pull out of The Snortery, and the men Schmitty had stationed along the bar had stopped them.

I had been fooled, but I must plead that I had neither Rudy's expertise in wigs and makeup nor Inspector Schmidt's penetrating eye. I had seen the Gus Rogers mug shot. I had even studied it. I don't think it was the switch to the blond wig that had thrown me off. It was the lip makeup and the eyelashes. He might that night have been looking recognizably like the big redhead. To me he had looked nothing like Gus Rogers.

Inspector Schmidt stepped into the melee.

"You can stow it away," he said. "Gus Rogers and Jake Malone, I'm putting you both under arrest."

He began reading them their rights, but the man he'd called Malone interrupted. I'd heard of Malone, but I'd never seen him. It was just that the word had been around that Malone had come to town and that he looked as though he might be trying to build himself a crime empire.

What with my connection with the inspector, I know a lot of cops. I get to hear things like that.

"Me?" Malone was saying. "Why me? You've got nothing on me."

"You," the inspector said. "You're the missing piece." He shoved them toward his waiting men. "Move them along," he said, and he read them their rights on the way out.

It was only when he'd seen the four of them booked and locked away and we were in his apartment and he had his shoes off and a proper drink in his hand that I got to ask my question.

"What was it with the missing piece?"

"It was a complicated job," Schmitty said, "but there was a touch of double cross in it that made it too complicated. Jim Marshall ran the operation. He had Maryjane-margaret get Sterling back to New York and introduce him to P.J.'s."

"So that when it was done, in the event that it didn't go down as a sex deal, everything would point to Cal Williams," I said.

"Yes. Williams would be a good fall guy, and Marshall liked the idea of punishing Williams."

"For what?"

"Cal Williams was out and he wasn't playing along. A man shouldn't be allowed to do that and get away with it. Once a guy belongs to Jim Marshall, it's for life. Marshall, if he can help it, tolerates nothing less."

The way Schmitty explained it, it had been a well-designed operation that should have worked. Two things went wrong with it. One was the job Dick Warren did on Christopher Froman.

"That was just plain stupid," Schmitty said. "That's the trouble with running an operation at long distance. Marshall wasn't where he could keep it properly policed."

He didn't have to tell me what the other thing was.

"Doing it in Maryjanemargaret's apartment was the other thing," I said.

"Yes. That's where it made no sense. It couldn't be that Marshall would have pulled it that way to kill three birds with one stone. If he had any reason for wanting to get rid of the Warrens, he wouldn't have taken that way to do it. He would have just had them bumped. Doing it this way would have left them alive to talk, and you can't cross your own people and then expect they won't talk."

"And there's also the list of Marshall's visitors," I said. "There was nobody but the Warrens, and he could hardly have used them as messengers to carry the orders for their own destruction."

Inspector Schmidt grinned at me. "Good thinking," he said. "Any time you're ready to go on the cops, Baggy, I'll find a place for you."

Of course, I had to turn around and spoil it.

"But what about Cal Williams?" I said.

"What about him?"

"You couldn't believe that Cal Williams would do it that way to point the suspicion away from himself?"

"In cahoots with Maryjanemargaret? She was the one who planted Sterling in P.J.'s."

I shook my head. "It's dizzying," I said.

"I tried working it out for it's happening in the apartment being Sterling's own doing," Schmitty said. "He's scared but he's also in need. He picks up with Gusaugusta-gussie but he balks at going to his place with him or to any place they might have set up for it. He's scared of going places he can't be sure of. He insists on going home to his place."

"That's very possible," I said.

"Yes, but in that case it would have been just a roll in the hay and the main event left for another time when Gusaugustagussie would have won Sterling's trust. I couldn't get that one to jell."

He left it there and he turned to Maryjanemargaret's great anger. In the morning when we had seen her up the river she had been in a rage, but it hadn't been because her lover had been murdered. That she had expected since she had set him up for it. What she hadn't been expecting was that it would have been done in her apartment. She had been put into jeopardy and she was furious.

"The baddies were Gusaugustagussie and Malone who was running him," the inspector said. "That's how we happened to luck into getting them all in the one bag tonight. Those two had been summoned to The Snortery, and they were going to be dealt with. We turned up and saved them from that."

"Both of them dealt with because Gusaugustagussie had been stupid?"

"Not stupid," Schmitty said. "Acting under orders. Do it in her place. The fuzz will grab the Warrens, and Marshall gets a sentence piled on to what he's now serving that'll have him coming out in the term of some President whose old man hasn't even been born yet. Malone then has a clear field for taking over everything that Jim Marshall has had going."

"The missing piece."

"As soon as I saw him with Gusaugustagussie, the whole thing sewed itself up," Inspector Schmidt said.

"Can you believe it was the great love that brought Ster-. ling back?" I asked.

"More likely she had him thinking he was being taken back into the fold. He was vain enough and stupid enough. She could have sold him the idea that he was such a great operator that they couldn't do without him."

"If he'd bought that, what was he afraid of?"

"He was waiting to be sure. Something like being given his first assignment would have made him sure. You must remember the man was an idiot. If you want to understand a Jack Sterling, you have to practice up on thinking like an idiot."

I freshened up Inspector Schmidt's drink. He wiggled his toes.

George Bagby is the pen name of an author who has been honored with the Grand Master Award, the Mystery Writers of America's highest distinction. He has been writing crime novels since 1935. He was born in Manhattan and has always lived there (when not on world travels), and New York City plays an important role in nearly all his George Bagby novels. The most recent adventures of Bagby and his mentor, Inspector Schmidt, include *A Question of Quarry, Country and Fatal, Mugger's Day,* and *I Could Have Died.*